ACTION AT WAR BOW VALLEY

ACTION AT WAR BOW VALLEY

MICHAEL CARDER

CUTTING EDGE

Paperback ISBN-13: 978-1-957868-16-5

Published by
Cutting Edge Books
PO Box 8212
Calabasas, CA 91372
www.cuttingedgebooks.com

ACTION AT WAR
BOW VALLEY

CHAPTER ONE

LATE APRIL RAINS had drenched the country for a week. From the Medicine Hills eastward to the Bowstring Range, the land lay sodden and bemired. A cold that had begun with last night's dusk had grown through the drizzly hours of darkness, and now its sharp edge ran through the day, turning the rain into occasional squalls of wet snow and laying a mushy skim of ice at the edge of the water that lay pooled in the hollows of the land.

Jim Embree, riding down the backbone of the Medicines, sat hunched in the saddle, chilled to the bone in spite of his sheepskin and its covering slicker. A gray depression compounded his physical misery, for since leaving the ranch an hour ago he had found three new Spanish Spur calves dead, their mothers hovering dumbly near. This weather would take its toll of the spring calf crop, another blow following that of last year's disastrous die-up, and, altogether, a gloomy prospect for his boss, Cal Sutton.

Embree tried to force his thoughts away from these facts, as being of no direct concern to him; and could not. The prospects facing Sutton were grim ones, and Embree felt a kind of pity settle in him as he thought of Sutton back at the ranch, fighting a twisting rheumatism that had chained him to a chair most of the winter, and now, in the spring, staring hopelessly into gray skies that would not clear.

He shifted his tall frame stiffly in the saddle, his slicker making a brittle crackling sound as he flexed the muscles of his heavy shoulders against the chill cramping them. He was a tanned wiry young man in his mid-twenties, with hair as jet-black as an

Indian's and eyes equally dark and piercing. Some inner unrest seemed always to move behind those eyes, even at times such as now, when a characteristic slow thoughtfulness lay on their surface, giving his regular, handsome features a soberness, a deliberation going beyond his years; and at this moment this seeming paradox of his nature was most apparent.

Down the pine-timbered slopes below him, mist rose thinly through the trees, and somewhere a rain-swollen rivulent, ordinarily gentle, brawled down its course. Water dripped on Embree from stark branches over the trail, branches whose newly budded miniatures of leaves seemed dormant and discouraged in this spring day's rawness. His horse plodded on, its hoofs sucking at the slippery footing and a rank warm steam rising from its drenched hide to linger in Embree's nostrils.

Some time later the trail bore to the right, dropping as it curved into the westward thrust of the Medicine Hills, and after some minutes it ran out upon a scarred, sparsely timbered flank of the hills. Open space lay before him. Embree reined in and halted.

War Bow Valley began at the bottom of this long grade, stretching off to the line of broken hills which formed the boundary of Spanish Spur, and extending five miles in the other direction toward the western boundary of Penn Drummond's D Slash. Once a reservation for Little Wolf's Sioux, War Bow Valley had been abandoned at some whim of the Washington politicians and the Indians moved to a permanent reservation farther north. Lying between Spanish Spur and D Slash range, it was used by both outfits for occasional graze, while the far western end had been thrown open by the government for homesteading and was being turned to crops by the farmers who had filed upon it.

Embree sat long, almost drowsily eyeing the smother of mist which clouded the Valley. In the middle distance, their lines smudged by haze, he saw the ruins of the old Post: the commandant's building, the sutler's store, the old commissary. Gone to ruin these two decades, they were now mere reminders that this was still government property.

Thinking that, Embree turned to look directly ahead, across the muddy churning waters of Buffalo Creek, which crossed the Valley and angled over into the southern section of Spanish Spur. Three miles across the way, the hills rose in irregular steps and broken pine-covered contours to the boundary of Penn Drummond's high graze. It was all a vast and fateful panorama, for here he had the clear picture of the antagonistic forces bearing in upon this tract: the farmers, Penn Drummond, and Spanish Spur, all needing the Valley, all reaching for it, none sure of it.

Reflectively, Embree took this into his mind, and then the sobering reason for his being out in this foul morning came back to him, and he lifted the reins and headed into the downward trail, his dark eyes somber under his forward-tilted hatbrim, his long mouth thoughtfully pursed.

On the valley floor, Embree forded Buffalo Creek and cut out to the southeast, letting his horse go at an easy canter. He was almost upon the fringe of hills where Spanish Spur and D Slash joined boundaries when he heard a halloo behind him. Reining in a little, he turned in the saddle and saw a rider coming up the road from the farmers' end of the Valley. It was Tom Houghton, one of the nesters.

Houghton brought his horse up beside Embree, grining cheerfully in spite of the foul weather. "I thought it was you," he said. "Mind if I ride along to town?"

Embree returned the smile, briefly showing strong white teeth. "Glad to have your company," he said cordially, and turned his horse to the road.

As they rode along, chatting inconsequentially, Embree found himself thinking of the pressure which had developed against these farmers, a pressure which, once purely social, now threatened to become violently personal. Under its force, most of the hoemen had turned bitter and resentful. Young Houghton, however, maintained an even good humor to all, meeting the baiting of the cattlemen with an easy laugh or smile, betraying none of the annoyance which their jibes aroused in him. It was a quality that Embree liked. Even now, Houghton's friendly grin seemed to make the day somehow better.

Presently there came a lull in the conversation, and Houghton remarked offhandedly, "If you'd rather, I'll leave you at the edge of town."

"Only if you want to. Don't do it for me."

Houghton turned to Embree, his pleasant face sobered. "Thanks. It's just that I thought it might not be too good for you." And he added bitterly, "Penn Drummond and his bunch might not take too kindly to your being with a farmer today."

"I work for Cal Sutton." A faint irritation edged Embree's soft Texas drawl. "Drummond's opinions mean nothing to me."

"A nice way to be. But after today, I guess every farmer in the Valley will hear every word Drummond says—and pay attention."

The rueful tone, and the respectful awe it implied, stirred up an old perverseness in Embree, but after a moment he merely replied, "That could be," and left it like that, holding his clear impression of trouble ahead.

Since riding up from Texas on the loose two years ago to take Cal Sutton's offer of the job as foreman of Spanish Spur, he had seen the shaping-up of this country's animosities. The pattern had been both inexorable and familiar: the slow encroachments of the farmers meeting Penn Drummond's hungry drive for land and power, with Spanish Spur and the other outfits undecided, sympathizing with the farmers but reluctant to take sides openly, and, hence, being drawn closer to the conflict. And now it had become clear that a balance had to be struck, for the land in dispute was the last of the public land, and to every interested faction it was either a necessary or an ardently desired prize.

Today, he realized, would probably lay down a course for the future; and he wondered, as he had been doing for some time in the past, what his own place would be in what surely was to come. In his pocket was Joe Morrissey's last letter, asking him to come to Alamogordo and go partners in a horse ranch. It was tempting: friends of a hundred campfires, they had ridden north from Texas together in pursuit of that very dream. And yet, there was Cal Sutton, sick and losing out, whom he liked and respected. When a man rode for a brand, he stayed with it through the hard times, and if he left it, he did so only when things were going well and he could look without a twinge of conscience down a trail he had never ridden before.

It might have been different, he argued with himself, if young Brad Sutton had been even a little like his sister, Amy. For, while the boy spent his time in town, drinking too much and gambling, Amy—and he thought of this with a strange secret warmth—had this year gone back to teaching school in order to help her father make ends meet. She was of Cal Sutton's cut and temper. And, reason it as he would, Embree felt bound to them by a loyalty that had a lot to do with the way they had waged a losing fight. Perhaps, after all, there was no hurry about Joe's offer. He would wait and see....

They came presently to another road, followed it a distance, and, topping a small rise in the last line of hills, abruptly saw the town off in the distance—a dirty gray smudge against the piled-up haze, a cluster of houses and buildings whose outlines were partially veiled by the curtain of rain before them. Then, as they dropped down to the intervening two miles of flatland, Embree spied the rider on the road ahead.

He had a strange reaction as the man turned in the saddle and looked back, for he recognized the long buffalo coat and flat-brimmed gray hat of Sam Arnim. Arnim halted and waited, greeted Embree civilly and nodded to Houghton, then rode on abreast of them.

Embree felt in this man's presence a reserved dislike which, he admitted, might be unfair to Arnim. Therefore, he tolerated him, knowing that Arnim both sensed and returned his sentiments. The fact that Cal Sutton had accepted Arnim as a likely choice for Amy's husband had nothing to do with his feeling, he believed, but while the fact should have been a recommendation, he found that it was not.

"A fine spring day," Arnim grumbled disgustedly.

"For ducks and Indians."

"Or rustlers?"

The unexpected malice of the question brought Embree's gaze to Arnim quickly, but Arnim was watching Houghton's reaction. Houghton kept his face straight ahead, guarding silence. A hard mischief was on Arnim's square face, and his slate-gray eyes were very still as he insisted, "How about it, Tom?"

Houghton asked, "The weather?"

"You know what," Arnim said pointedly.

The farmer turned then. "I wouldn't know." His smile seemed a bit strained. "My business is farming."

"Ah! Maybe it was, but if that jury convicts Meeker today, there's going to be a lot of land for sale down the Valley."

"Not mine," said Houghton, still with good humor.

Arnim grunted. "You think that Drummond will let you fellows stay down there, killing his beef and pushing in on his graze? Tell me another!"

Embree had not welcomed the prospect of riding to town with Sam Arnim, and now the man's words both startled and angered him; the young farmer hadn't asked for this needling.

Making an honest effort at civility, he said gruffly, "Lay off, Sam. Meeker's the one on trial. Besides, War Bow isn't Drummond's graze."

Arnim gave him a quick straight look, then faced around, saying with complete conviction, "Every farmer in the Valley is on trial—make no mistake about that. And if the Valley isn't Drummond's yet, it will be."

"You seem mighty certain of that."

Arnim seemed to think that over for a space. He was a big-framed man, yellow-haired, with a not unpleasant face. But a bullish mood was on him that seemed to rub up friction between himself and Embree.

"I'm a realist," he said finally, staring straight ahead. "Cal Sutton was the only man big enough to hold Drummond back. But he can't buck him now, and Drummond knows that. He also knows if he gets his hands on War Bow, he'll control the water for a good third of Sutton's best graze. This time next year, if you're still around, you'll see that Sutton's been pushed back to the hill graze. Then—good-by, Spanish Spur!"

This indifferent voicing of Spanish Spur's troubles raised a slow anger in Embree, but he put it down, saying coldly, "He's got to buy War Bow Valley at public auction. There's no guarantee he'll get it."

"Don't worry, he will." Then Arnim added, with some conviction, "None of us can stop Drummond. Why are we headed for town right now? Because whether or not they convict that rustler, Drummond will have his way."

"Will Meeker's no rustler!" Houghton had stood enough. Now he faced Arnim, a weary anger in his voice as he said, "Meeker would have paid for that beef. He did no worse than I've done myself. Embree here told us all we could kill an occasional cow, if we'd just drive back his drift now and then."

Arnim's jaw dropped. He turned and met Embree's straight hard stare a moment, and then he looked away, saying disgustedly, "No wonder they slaughter our beef! By God, Penn's right about this!"

His defense of Drummond had strained Embree's already thin patience. "Yeah," he drawled, with searing sarcasm.

"Drummond couldn't be wrong. If a farmer's family gets hungry and he kills a beef, send him to jail! That'll fill their bellies."

Arnim said nothing to that for a moment, and then he replied stubbornly, "I may sound like that, but Drummond's got something——"

"Drummond be damned!" Embree suddenly flared. "He speaks, and everybody jumps. He's so high and mighty that nobody will stand up to him. It's sickening! What's so special about him?"

Arnim turned, sobered by Embree's vehemence, and looked at him intently. Then, tight-lipped, he turned away. "Nothing special, but whether you like it or not he's running this country.'

"The hell he is!" Embree raged quietly. "He's not running me, and he's not running Spanish Spur. He's bought himself a sheriff, and he makes the bank do handsprings, and somehow he's convinced men who ought to know better that he's unbeatable. But that doesn't make him God—not yet."

"Oh, damn it, tell him that!" Arnim retorted. Then, his anger going, he added defensively, "It's not my fault—I just face facts."

"Facts? You're quick-tongued enough to sell out the farmers and Spanish Spur, but if we go, you'll be next. There's your facts."

Arnim's face changed color, but he shook his head. "Drummond will never tackle Box A. He knows I'll let him alone, and he couldn't take us if he tried."

"Ah," said Embree. He was about to add something to that, but he changed his mind. Arnim was wrong, but he was stubborn, and this was a useless argument. He said, "Anyhow, Cal Sutton won't be as easy as Drummond may think."

"Why, I hope that's so," said Arnim. And then he added doggedly, "But I still think it's too big a load for Cal—and you."

"We'll handle it." Embree made it quietly final. Thus it rested as they rode into town.

The town of Wells lay in the broad hollow of the prairie, facing the sunrise over a westward-curving finger of the Bowstring

Range. To the north and west the grass ran in an undulating sweep to the Hills bordering War Bow Valley and the Medicines north of it. The town lay in the center of the ranges, all roads converged upon it, and the ranches, the shipping pens, and the railroad gave it its life—a life which at this moment was changing.

Arnim left them as they turned into the length of Main Street, whose dust was now a churned-up sea of mud. Embree's gaze ran down the row of angular false-fronted buildings forming the heart of the town. Horses lined the racks, their hair tufted with rain, their bellies and legs plastered with mud. At the far end of the street he saw the jumble of nesters' wagons hitched near the Apex freight yard. Men conversed in small knots back under the stores' wooden awnings, and at the crossing of Main and Railroad a large group of cattlemen waited patiently in the rain, ill-sheltered by the bare cottonwoods before the courthouse. Meeker's trial, Embree saw, was still in progress.

Embree pulled into the rack before the saloon, waving casually to Houghton who rode on downstreet. He got down, tied, and stood in the deep mud, filling his pipe and tamping the tobacco down with some care, while his eyes soberly assessed the street. The rain hissed softly into the pooled ruts, it pattered on his slicker, and it muted the distant voices of men without obliterating the hushed tension in their voices. The damp smell of soaked unpainted wood, of horses, of the drowned earth and the freshness of distant grasslands was in his nostrils.

He observed all these phenomena with some care: among the men in this street were his enemies and his friends; others yet could be one or the other. But he was certain that a line would soon be drawn, and, knowing the full meaning of both friendship and enmity in a hot-tempered land, he made this careful, aloof appraisal. Then he ducked under the tie-up and headed for the saloon.

On the plank walk he paused to stomp the mud from his boots, then struck a match to his pipe. Frank Moore-head and

Stacey Jennings broke from a group before the hotel and came up toward him, their boots striking dully on the walk. They gave him sober greeting, and for a space they swapped idle gossip. Moorehead and Jennings were small ranchers from over in the Lobos, neighbors of Cal Sutton. They were natives of the country, which Embree was not, they liked him and valued his judgment, and he knew that they were drawn to him by the hope that he could answer a question.

Embree asked, "What's the latest on Meeker?"

"As you know, the jury hung up last night," Jennings told him. "Judge Mortler told 'em if they didn't arrive at a verdict by noon, he'd discharge 'em." He made a grimace. "They've got a half hour to go."

There was a brief silence. Then Moorehead suggested, "It's warmer in the bar. Let's go in." They turned into the saloon.

The bar was lined and all tables were occupied. Embree glimpsed Sam Arnim down the way, and then his eye picked out some of Drummond's D Slash riders clustered together toward the rear. He saw no farmers here.

They ordered whiskey and, when it came, raised their glasses gravely to one another and drank. The talk at the bar was subdued, tentative. Suddenly Embree thought, they're all waiting for a verdict they already know.

Beside him, Moorehead was complaining, "It's the town people and a farmer or two who's hung the jury. Still, all considered, there's not much room for argument. They caught Meeker skinning out a D Slash steer on Drummond's range." He paused, demanded peevishly, "Why the hell don't they finish it up?"

"Maybe they don't think it's that simple," Embree said quietly.

"But it ought to be plain enough. If they don't send Meeker to the pen, what's the use of a law?"

"Yet he claimed he'd of paid off," Jennings objected, troubled.

"Paid, hell! They all say that—after they're caught. This time it was Drummond; next time, maybe you, maybe me. And it was a Drummond beef, no doubt—they've got the hide for evidence." He gave Embree a slanting, questioning stare. "What do you think, Embree?"

"Poor Drummond," Embree drawled.

They both looked at him quickly, catching the sarcasm, and then their eyes met gravely. Slowly, Jennings set his glass down on the wood. "Yeah," he said with soft irony. "A shame about Drummond. But we'd better make up our minds how much our hearts bleed for him—and do it now."

"How's that?" Moorehead queried instantly.

"Why dammit, Frank, you know they're laying bets that Meeker won't leave town alive—convicted or not."

Embree heard this with a deep shock and alarm. A slow dread settled into him as he got the full implication of Jennings' words.

"Who's offering the money?" he asked softly.

"Who? D Slash, of course!" Then Jennings added with low outrage, "Drummond's gunmen are in town—Bob Hackett and that drifter they call Taos."

Embree nodded, pulling deep on his pipe. He stared straight ahead, but his narrowed eyes grew harder.

Jennings amplified his statement. "Drummond's getting too big for his britches. I'm against killing another man's beef, but I'm also for a fair trial and stick by the verdict."

Again, Moorehead glanced uneasily at Embree. "Look," he said, after a moment. "You're foreman of the next biggest outfit to Drummond. Maybe Stacey here's right—maybe D Slash is going too far. What have us little fellows got to do, Embree?"

Embree deliberately knocked the dottle from his pipe and put it in his pocket. He distrusted any man who could not by now have arrived at an attitude in this matter. With a slow shake of his head he said, utterly neutral, "At times like this a man has to make his own decisions. If you can't make up your own mind, why ask me?"

They gave him a blank unsatisfied look, and then some other men came in the door and these two drifted away. Embree thought, at least Jennings knows the answer, and filed that fact away in his mind.

He stood leaning idly on the wood, thinking over what they had said. He was thus preoccupied when Sam Arnim cruised down toward him and elbowed up to the bar.

"I'll buy you a drink," Arnim offered.

"Thanks, but I've had one." Then, not wanting to reject Arnim's gesture of peace, he countered, "Let me buy yours."

Arnim nodded and waved to the bartender. He took a sip of his drink and faced Embree. "How's Cal?"

"About the same—pretty well tied down to his chair."

"It's too bad," Arnim said earnestly. "I'm really sorry for him."

His mood had changed, although there was still in him a trace of the stiffness he always showed Embree. Studying him, Embree pondered the thing that always put them at cross purposes, like two strange dogs raising their hackles and growling at one another. At times like the present, Arnim was a pleasant enough man, but such times were rare, and in a way Embree was sorry that it was so.

Arnim said, temporizingly, "I guess I was a little snappish a while ago. I may have sounded a way I didn't mean."

"Forget it. Everybody's a little upset by this thing."

"Just so." But something deeper was bothering Arnim. He said with some care, "I just don't want to give the impression that I'm against Spanish Spur. Cal Sutton is my friend. And he has a fine girl in Amy." Then, turning his gaze squarely at Embree, "I don't suppose it's any secret to you that I intend to marry her someday."

"No, it's no secret."

"Good. Maybe we understand each other." Arnim stared down at the bar a moment before he added with stubborn conviction, "But I'll believe I'm right about this situation until I'm proved wrong. And I think you'd do well to get Cal Sutton to make his peace with Penn Drummond."

"On Drummond's terms?" Embree asked ironically. "Maybe you'd better change your ideas, Arnim. You may need Spanish Spur someday yourself."

Doggedly, Arnim shook his head. He was about to offer his rebuttal when the swing doors burst open and a puncher stuck his head inside and yelped, "Jury's comin' in!"

An excited commotion of voices and scuffling boots and scraping chairs rose up, and the crowd pushed toward the doors past Embree. He waited until the bar had cleared, then started out, and at that moment he spied Brad Sutton sitting alone at a back table, where he had been shielded by the crowd. Turning, Embree went back that way.

Brad watched his approach with a dark resentful stare. A stubble of beard blurred Brad's thin, sharply handsome face, and a looseness about his mouth told Embree that he had been drinking too much. Embree paused by the table, looking down at him.

"You'll never find it there," he said.

"What?" Brad demanded.

"They don't put answers in whiskey bottles—just whiskey."

Brad hesitated, then said with considerable precision. "Embree, how about minding your own business?"

"It's my business that your father's poorly. I don't mind telling you that business would be better if you showed up at home now and then."

"No," Brad shook his head. "Stick to cow talk, and I'll listen."

Suddenly Embree leaned across the table, saying low and hard, "You listen to me, or, by Godfrey, you'll wish you had! Your father's in trouble, and your sister's working because you won't. At least you owe them the satisfaction of seeing you. Now get this : if you're not at home this evening by suppertime, I'm coming to town and drag you out at a rope's end!"

Brad colored but could not meet the contempt in Embree's sharp gaze. He looked away, and then, before he could reply, Embree wheeled and went out through the saloon to the street.

Down near the cottonwoods of the courthouse he saw the D Slash riders clustered about Penn Drummond. Drummond's tall frame stood a head higher than the others, and he was speaking energetically, his dark head bobbing, his beefy arms slashing the air with almost physical violence. Suddenly he pointed across the street, and Embree saw a score of farmers move out into the street's mud and halt. They planted themselves doggedly before Drummond and his bunch, eyeing them with a sullen determination.

The rain had slacked off to a drizzle. Behind the nesters, townsmen stood before the stores under the wooden awnings' overhang. Embree moved on, past the harness shop, the feed store, halting at last on the boardwalk's edge where he could see both the farmers and Drummond's crowd over the way. Penn Drummond raised his eyes, looked straight at Embree for a moment; then he turned toward the courthouse.

Embree weighed this scene with all his attention. Some of the smaller ranchers now joined Drummond's group, Frank Moorehead being one of them. They had fallen silent, and everyone was watching the courthouse intently. A tension grew in the street, catching at Embree's nerves. Then the courthouse door opened, a slickered puncher appeared, paused a moment to make a two-handed semaphore of negation and disgust, and then came down to join the D Slash crowd. A low murmur of approval went up from the homesteaders, but Penn Drummond wheeled toward the sound and a man lifted his hand and it subsided.

Then Will Meeker, who had butchered a D Slash steer and now was free by the jury's finding, stepped out of the courthouse door, looked quickly around the street, and stopped dead still.

CHAPTER TWO

A LL SOUND had been sucked out of the street, leaving utter stillness. Drummond slowly moved a little to one side, leaving the way clear before the courthouse steps, and his men shifted likewise, their faces remaining turned toward Meeker. Out of the corner of his eye, Embree caught a movement, and turning, he saw Tom Houghton push, grim-faced, to the front of the group of farmers.

These shiftings, this movement, had their meaning, and Embree read it; then he turned to observe Meeker, who stood pale and taut, looking toward the farmers, and then, for a brief moment, apprehensively at the cattlemen. He was a stringy man in bib overalls and a faded jumper under a disheveled coat that was too large for him. An odd mixture of defiance and fear was on his face as he looked over the street, point by point; then he drew up his thin shoulders and moved down the steps.

Coming abreast of Drummond, Meeker turned, showing the gray bitterness of his face; afterward, relief lighting his eyes, he glanced back toward his own people. Drummond and his men followed Meeker's progress with unveiled contempt, pivoting slowly as he went on. Reaching the boardwalk's margin, Meeker paused momentarily; he was almost smiling now. Then, as he stepped down into the street, the flat sharp crack of a rifle, coming from somewhere upstreet, shattered the silence.

For a split second no one moved. Will Meeker halted sharply, his face jerking up with a panicky bafflement fleeting over it. He seemed to rise a little on his toes as though against a weight bearing him down overpoweringly. Then all expression left his face, his knees folded, and he toppled forward into the mud.

Those along the street watched this with a morbid fascination. Embree was stubbornly refusing to believe it, even while the hot outrage flooded up in him. He heard the homesteaders react with a deep growl of shocked fury, but he was watching the way Drummond's men immediately fanned out across the walk, reaching for their guns.

Drummond's harsh voice rapped out. "Hold fast, there! Start something and there'll be more of the same!"

Embree was thinking bleakly, he had a rifle planted in the hotel's second story. The heartless calculation of it, the hard insolence that had come into Drummond's round-jawed bulldog face, hit him with a sickening disgust.

The farmers seemed stunned. And on their faces was a fear, an awed respect for Penn Drummond's power that held them rooted and made them less than men.

Drummond, seeing this, warned arrogantly, "Move and you move into a fight. Meeker got what any cow-killer deserves." And none of them challenged the scornful intolerance of his tone.

Tom Houghton moved forward.

Drummond at once swung toward him. "Houghton, you heard me!"

The farmer plodded on over the mud, his face pinched and bitter. "Go ahead and shoot," he said wearily. "I've got no gun either."

The group about Drummond shifted uneasily; they had holstered their guns and were not quite sure. Then Drummond made a brief signal and stepped over near Meeker's body where it lay in the slow drizzle.

"What do you want, Houghton?"

Houghton said nothing at once. He had halted two paces from the dead man and was staring down at him. Then, slowly, he glanced back at the farmers. They had faded out of the street and back into the crowd, and he was alone. He turned a bleak face to Drummond.

"He can't just lay there," he said dismally. "In the mud like this—"

Drummond hesitated, then interpreted this as a challenge. "He'll lay there until Doc Noble comes after him. This thing is going on the coroner's records straight."

Houghton seemed not to understand. "But his wife's sick," he said, almost mildly. "It's only decent to take him home."

"He stays here until Doc comes," Drummond repeated flatly.

"Penn," said a man behind Drummond, in a dubious tone, "Doc Noble went out of town this morning on a call."

But Drummond could not back down now. Anger threw his rocky jaw out a little farther. "He'll be back. And you shut up!" he snapped. Then, to Houghton, "Beat it. We'll handle this and anything else that might come up."

He raised his head, glaring across the street, and spoke to anyone and everyone who had witnessed this and seen him in a bad light. "This is cow country. It's going to stay that way, and you farmers had better get that in your heads. Now—clear out! Meeker'll be taken care of."

Every soul in the street knew that Drummond's words had publicly reversed the jury's verdict, that he was challenging anyone to disagree with his decision. Yet Houghton said stubbornly, "Let the Doc come down the Valley. I'll take Meeker to his folks."

Embree, on the boardwalk, saw the dogged determination on the young farmer's face, and he saw Drummond run a quick glance over the crowd and then make up his mind. Drummond took a small step forward, asking thinly, "Have I got to teach you a lesson, Houghton?"

The anger tightened in Embree all at once. He knew then that he would stand by Houghton if Drummond moved. Sober judgment told him that the time had passed for thinking of whether a man ran cows or raised wheat; it became more remote with every second that the dead man lay huddled there in the mud and rain.

Even as this strong revulsion hit Embree, Houghton said with low fury, "Just try it! Try and teach me a lesson, damn you!"

Without warning, Drummond lurched past Meeker's body and swung a wicked blow full upon Houghton's jaw. Houghton, taken by surprise, reeled backward and fell to one knee as Embree, driven by outraged instinct, came down off the walk at a half run.

He reached Drummond as the big man was advancing on Houghton, his eyes glittering with rage. Embree called sharply, "Drummond—here!" and as the man wheeled, Embree's left fist came up and caught him on the shoulder, whirling him full around.

At the same moment there was a flurry on the boardwalk, and a Drummond man clawed aside his slicker and reached for his gun. Down the way Stacey Jennings' wintry voice warned, "Don't do that!" and the man looked into the muzzle of Jennings' gun and changed his mind.

"Just everybody be calm," Jennings cautioned gently.

Drummond had come to a skidding halt, his feet wide-planted, his head lowered bullishly as he glowered at Embree.

Embree had pushed back his slicker a little, freeing the gun on his thigh. For a moment he stared straight at Drummond before he drawled softly, "You won your bet on Meeker, and now I'll make you one: I'll bet you we take Meeker down the Valley. Want to call it, Drummond?"

The challenge was almost gentle, but it was deadly and unexpected, and it seemed to deepen the stillness. Then a snarling voice on the boardwalk said, "Why, damn him! Nobody lays it down to D Slash like that. Nobody!"

"Shut up, Taos," Jennings growled.

An anger past voicing had flushed Drummond's heavy face a dark-stained red. He seemed on the point of some violent explosion. As Houghton picked himself up, Drummond shot him a glance, and then his face changed and he turned to study Embree.

"So you're siding with the nesters," he said, with grim finality.

Embree ignored that, saying to Houghton, "Go fetch a wagon, Tom. I'll help you with Meeker." Houghton hesitated only a moment, then strode away.

Everyone was waiting, a kind of stunned wonder over them, for Drummond to act. No man could pass up such things as Embree had laid against him here, publicly, unequivocally.

But after his hesitation, Drummond merely turned away and tramped past the form of Meeker to the boardwalk, where he once more squared around, facing the street. The flame of his anger brightened his eyes, but his voice was tight and controlled as he said, "I've got other things for a while, Embree. But when they're done, I'll see you. In the meantime, I'll consider you and Spanish Spur as one with the nesters."

"Do so," said Embree shortly. After an instant he turned on his heel and went up the street, through an astonished silence. He came to the hitchrack, slipped the reins, and pulled up into the saddle. Sam Arnim came up the walk and paused before him, face face wearing a moody soberness.

"Well," Arnim said, "that did it."

"Did it, now?" Embree mocked dryly.

"You're damn right it did. If I was Cal Sutton, by the Lord Harry, I'd fire you."

"But you're not." Embree reined out and rode down the street.

Houghton was there with a farmer's wagon. They lifted Meeker's body out of the mud, a curious few morbidly watching them, laid it in the wagon bed, and covered it with a tarpaulin. Then Houghton tied his horse to the endgate and climbed to the seat. As he lifted the reins he turned. "You don't have to come, Embree."

"I'm going along. Get moving."

They went down the street, the horses splashing noisily through the hock-deep mire.

The town, Embree knew, was watching them go, forming its judgments and establishing its peculiar loyalties after what had happened today. There was no longer any doubt: Penn Drummond stood against all others whose existence depended upon War Bow Valley. Law or no law, Drummond would fight for the Valley, and the devil take the weaker man.

Before the hotel, Drummond and his two gunmen, Hackett and Taos, stood back under the awning. As the wagon passed, bearing the murdered homesteader, these men watched with a steady unwavering hostility, their gazes holding fast upon Embree. He gave them a long, piercing glance, and rode on.

All this morning, Amy Sutton had gone about her classroom duties mechanically, secretly preoccupied by a dread of what the outcome of the Meeker affair might mean for her father and Spanish Spur. Now, as she taught the reading class of fifth graders, she was scarcely able to concentrate on the halting, labored recitations; her thoughts were on her father: ill, brooding over his own helplessness, shamed and proud at once for her working, and worried about Brad.

Without condemning Brad, Amy, too, wished that he would do better, that he might shoulder some of the load. In spite of his faults, she still loved him, but at times such as today, when there seemed no clear path ahead, Amy realized that Brad's erratic ways were depriving her father of a needed comfort and support ....

All at once she became aware that a little girl who had been reading had finished her passage for recitation, had sat down, and was staring at her. Covering her embarrassment, Amy called a study period and went to stand by the window, frowning out at the gaunt locusts rimming the mud-and-cinder schoolyard.

The report of a gun, coming muted and hollow from the direction of the town's center, jerked her back to reality. She tensed, then wheeled just as a buzzing excitement rose among the pupils and an older boy said aloud, with mock sadness, "Well, there goes poor Meeker!"

Furious that this thing had been brought home even to the children, Amy rang the bell for recess, even though it lacked fifteen minutes of noon. She slowed the rush out of doors, making sure that the children were properly dressed; then, her mind in a turmoil, she went to her desk and opened her lunch. She was toying with a tasteless sandwich when she spied through the steamy window a wagon coming out from town and, following it, a rider whom she presently recognized as Embree. She pushed back her chair and rose, walking rapidly to the front.

As Amy stepped outside to greet him, Embree waved the wagon on and reined in toward the porch, touching his hat to her and eyeing her gravely.

She was a tall slender girl, with hair the color of ripe wheat and eyes as blue as the sky over the mountaintops on a cloudless day. Her face was delicate, yet strong-featured, and as she looked up at Embree her blue eyes were troubled and her long full lips soberly drawn.

He saw her worry and said, with soft regret, "Amy, there's been trouble in town."

"I guessed as much when I heard the shot. Was it Meeker?"

Embree nodded. "The jury cleared him, but when he came out of the courthouse somebody shot him from ambush." He turned and waved toward the wagon lumbering down the road. "There he goes—poor devil."

She stood a long moment looking after the wagon and he saw her mouth draw a little tighter at the corners. Then she turned back to him. "So they dared to do it," she breathed.

"A warning of what we can expect," he told her. He hesitated a moment before saying, "It strikes me that this news won't do your father any good. Would you mind going home for tonight? I'm going down the Valley with Houghton now, but I'll be out later."

He was asking this for her father; and, knowing that, it came to her that she had learned something strange about this man: just talking to him, seeing him and hearing his soft unhurried drawl, bolstered her feelings. Without realizing it, she had come to depend upon him in many ways since her father's sickness. During the two years that he had been at Spanish Spur, their relationship had been casual, rather distant, for he had always kept his distance, eating with the crew and riding the range for long periods as his work demanded, so that actually, she realized, she scarcely knew him. Yet, somehow, this fuller appreciation of him had grown, this certainty of his strength and his sound judgment.

She said slowly, "Yes, I think I ought to be with Dad. I'll dismiss classes and go out this afternoon."

"That will be better," Embree agreed. Touching his hat again, he put his horse into motion and rode on at a canter after Houghton.

Amy stood looking after him a moment, then went in. After she had dismissed the delighted children she walked the short distance into town, going to the house her father maintained in Wells, where she stayed alone during the week. Arrived there, she changed into riding clothes, boots and a heavy jacket, and slipped on a slicker. Then, locking the door, she hurried down toward the livery stable.

John Strohmeyer, the hostler, brought her horse and held the bridle while Amy stepped up. "A foul day, Amy," he observed. "Not enough kids to hold classes?"

"Yes, there were," she replied, taking the reins from him. "But I sent them home. Hope the Board doesn't fire me."

He nodded, understanding. "You did right. I feel sorry for Cal, and I hope he doesn't get hurt too bad in this thing. Tell him I said hello."

"Thank you, John. I will." She rode out, turning north, and now her slow fear had turned into a conviction of some real trouble ahead. No farmer would be safe after this, and Drummond's drive would broaden to include anyone who used or needed War Bow Valley. That was why Embree had asked her to be with Cal Sutton today.

Outside the town Amy left the wagon road, going at a canter into the northwest, and holding the mist-shrouded shapes of the Medicines on her forward left. An hour later, in the timbered foothills, she struck a broad trail which soon topped out upon a long grassy mesa, and a short time later she rode into the ranch yard, noting at once that a horse bearing Sam Arnim's Box A brand was tied at the corral.

Amy got down and tied, and then walked slowly to the house, viewing with a deep good feeling the long low ranch house of log and stone, with its full veranda and the dark ragged screen of pines behind it. The sight never failed to stir her, and today she savored it doubly, knowing the danger which threatened Spanish Spur.

As Amy entered, Cal Sutton turned stiffly in his easy chair before the fireplace, and simultaneously Sam Arnim got to his feet, quick pleasure brightening his countenance.

Amy kissed her father on the forehead, gave Sam a friendly smile, and shed slicker and coat. Then, as she came toward the fire, Cal Sutton said, in his deep gruff-tender voice, "What's this, girl? Playing hooky?"

Amy turned to regard him. Sutton's frame was still that of a big man, his eyes the keen sharp blue of the fighter, but the broad shoulders were now a little stooped and his cheeks were pale and lined with worry, and with the old traces of pain silently borne.

"Not hooky, Dad," Amy said, with a tender smile. "I talked to Jim Embree, and he sent me out." She paused; then, sobering, said slowly, "Something happened in town today——"

"I know what happened," Sutton cut in abruptly. His face changed, and he turned his head away, looking into the fire. "Sam told me about it."

"I thought Cal ought to know, first off," Sam explained, as Amy shot him a glance. "After that fool trick of Embree's this whole thing has changed."

"What 'fool trick'?"

He stared at her: "He didn't tell you?"

"He said that Meeker had been killed."

"Ah," said Arnim ominously, "that's just the half of it." In a tone edged with resentment he recounted the fight between Houghton and Drummond, and the part which Embree had played by clashing with Drummond and laying down the challenge before him. "He only left Drummond one way to go," Arnim concluded indignantly, "and Cal here stands right in his path."

Amy watched Arnim intently as he spoke, and when he had finished she said in a slow, musing voice, "But he stood up for a poor devil who was trying to do the only decent thing."

Arnim's slate-gray eyes sharpened. "That's a matter of opinion," he said dryly. "Why force Drummond's hand at a time like this?"

She said nothing, but slowly swung around toward her father. Cal Sutton raised his head, a bitter reading of the future in his face, and he looked at Amy and then at Arnim and made a harsh resigned gesture. "No matter what we do, we stand in Drummond's way," he rumbled. "His killing of Meeker puts us all on notice that he's out to get what he wants and the law be damned. You or I could have been Meeker, Sam, and we may be yet."

"I can't believe that," Arnim said instantly.

"Then don't! But what Embree did changed nothing, except to bring things out in the open." Sutton paused, shaking his head heavily. "The worst of it is, this country could get along with the farmers, if it would. But Drummond had to have his excuse for a fight, and they were handy. One way or the other, he'd have gotten it anyhow."

"So what are you going to do?" Arnim asked.

Sutton was silent for some seconds, staring into the fire. Then he murmured perplexedly, "I wish I knew."

"And that's just my point, Cal," said Arnim softly. "Drummond holds the aces." He watched Sutton with a kind of pitying pessimism, and when the older man did not reply he sighed, reached for his hat, and said, "I'll be getting along. I hope you feel better, Cal."

Sutton merely raised a hand in farewell.

Amy walked to the porch with Arnim, and at the steps he paused, looking carefully into her face a moment before he asked, "I take it you agree with your father, Amy?"

"Yes. I wish that I had done what Embree did."

She was surprised to see the darkening of his face and the anger that lit up his eyes. She had not meant her words as a reproach, but she saw now that he had so taken them.

"So Embree's the big hero after today," Arnim said, low and bitter. "I didn't expect you to be impressed by it—especially since he was wrong to do it."

Amy was studying him with some wonder, telling herself that, though Sam was being unreasonable, still he was hurt. She scarcely knew how to answer, and after a moment she laughed lightly, saying, "Why, Sam, I believe you're jealous of him!"

As he colored, she knew that that had been the wrong thing to say. He was watching her steadily. "And would there be no reason for that, Amy?" he murmured.

She felt herself blushing now. "Why—why of course not! Embree has scarcely even looked at me!"

"Ah," said Sam. And then, slowly, he smiled one of his rare pleasing smiles. "I'm glad of that," he said softly. "And I hope you're right."

He went down the steps toward his horse, and presently he rode out of the yard. Amy watched him go; then, her eyes pensive, she went in to rejoin her father.

CHAPTER THREE

Penn Drummond stood glowering out of the window of his room on the hotel's second story, seeing nothing before him really, as he reviewed what had just happened. He was uncomfortably aware of the fact that the events at the courthouse had shown him up in a bad light; moreover, he believed that opposition to him would now form as a result of Embree's taking a hand in the matter, and he was not yet ready for that. He had let himself be drawn into a clumsy play, and it rankled.

All at once he wheeled and strode back across the room to the round center table where Hackett, sharp-faced and chill-eyed, lazily dealt showdown hands for himself and Taos, who was watching the cards with only mild interest.

"Put those cards away," Drummond growled. "You make me nervous."

Taos raised expressionless smoke-gray eyes, saying softly, "Then go see a doctor. Deal another, Bob."

Hackett laughed mockingly. "That fellow Embree got under your hide, didn't he, Drummond?'

"Certainly. I'd rather choose my own time to go into any game."

Hackett pushed the cards away and took out his makings. Regarding Drummond narrowly, he said, "Then raise right back at him."

"Meaning what?"

"You've got the nesters buffaloed, haven't you?"

"I think so."

Hackett finished his cigarette, lit it, and flipped the match away. "Then go after Sutton before he gets set. He's the one you want, anyhow."

Their eyes met, and a slow crafty smile spread over Drummond's face; then he nodded, pleased. "You're right—why not?" Again he moved to the window and stared out, his big chest rising and falling with some quick excitement. Suddenly he bobbed his close-cropped head and struck his fist into his palm with a sharp smack.

"Why, of course!" Grinning broadly he turned and came back to the table. "They won't expect us to move this soon—it would be natural to lie low for a while. So, we force the play." With sudden decision, he turned to Hackett. "Bob, you take a half dozen hands down through the Valley with you and tell those farmers I'm buying up any and all nester tracts. Hint to 'em that they're going to have to sell whether they want to or not. That'll give 'em something to worry about, and if you get any argument, well, you know what to do, don't you?"

Hackett rose, grinning lazily. "I'm of age," he said, and went out.

Taos was eyeing Drummond with complete cold neutrality. As Drummond turned to him, the gunman said contemptuously, "Don't ask me to burn any barns or pull farmers' whiskers, Drummond."

"No, I won't." Drummond took a cigar from his vest, bit off the end, and lit it. "You've got a little higher type of work ahead of you," he said, with thin irony. Taos waited.

"Down around the old Post in War Bow Valley, you'll find a lot of Sutton's cows and mine grazing together—all mixed up. I want you to take a crew and a wagon down there, this afternoon yet, and make a gather. Make it look like the real thing, understand?" And, as Taos nodded shortly, "There's a Spanish Spur line shack near there, and they're bound to investigate. When they do, you tell Sutton's men that we're pushing all the beef off the Valley—including Spanish Spur stuff. You get it?"

"I get it: they come in for their beef. Then what?"

"You don't have to let them take it, do you?" Drummond asked softly.

His expression unchanged, Taos got up and moved to the door. There he turned, asking dryly, "Who is it—that Embree fellow?"

Drummond ducked his head in affirmation. Without comment, Taos left.

For some seconds after his men had gone, Penn Drummond stood staring narrowly into space. Then he donned his long coat, clapped his hat on his head, and went down to the street, where he turned north along the boardwalk with a long purposeful stride. At the first intersection, he turned into a back street and shortly thereafter rapped brusquely on the door of a neat white-painted house set back on a lawn surrounded by a picket fence.

The woman who opened to his knock stood regarding him coolly, only a momentary flicker of her hazel eyes betraying her surprise.

"May I come in, Lily?" Drummond inquired.

After a brief hesitation she stepped aside and led the way down a hall to an interior room, brightly furnished, and here she faced him.

Lily Farnum at twenty-six had a mature woman's charm, along with a remnant of youth's freshness. She wore a dress of shiny blue stuff that brought out the rounded outlines of her body, and gleaming chestnut hair, piled high on her head, contrasted strikingly with her hazel eyes. Now she watched Drummond carefully and asked, in a cool tone, "What do you want?"

"Can't I at least sit down?" he protested.

"Not unless it's necessary," she replied calmly. "I do not like callers—there is enough gossip in this town about me as it is."

Drummond's eyes as he looked at her were at once resentful and admiring. In the five years since Lily Farnum had come to Wells, an attractive unattached girl, the gossip concerning her had failed completely to attach itself to substance. Some four or five businessmen, Drummond among them, knew that she had invested a small sum of money in the saloon and the feed store. These same men, too, grew aware as time passed that Lily Farnum was a sharp dealer in small transactions of the type considered honest only when carried out by men whose legitimate province is hardheaded business. And, as it became known that Lily had only a reserved comradeship to exchange for what men had to give, she was marked down as a lovely enigma, distrusted by the womenfolk for her beauty, and, for the same reason, quietly despaired of by the men.

Drummond was recalling all this as he murmured wryly, "Lily—the woman with the banker's heart. I wonder what you'd be like if——"

"I'm not interested in your daydreams. What do you want?"

"All right, all right!" he exclaimed irritably. He took a slow turn of the room and stopped before her. "You're seeing Brad Sutton, aren't you?"

She colored faintly, then replied, "Suppose I am?"

He pulled meditatively on his cigar, eyeing her the while. "Lily," he said finally, "I don't have to tell you what's going on in this place. It's going to come down to a fight between me and Sutton, and I want to keep a jump ahead of him, because I'm going to win, one way or the other!" He paused, then said quietly, "If you'd undertake to find out anything you can from Brad about their plans and pass the word on to me, I'd make it worth your while. What do you say?"

She said, "No. Will you leave now?"

He frowned, then suddenly he laughed. "I see your point—it looks like making a traitor out of Brad. But listen, Lily: there's not going to be any result of this that would cause him—or you either—a moment's regret."

"Do you suppose Meeker would agree with that?" she asked coldly.

He made an angry, impatient gesture. "I tell you, I'm not going to go after Sutton with guns! This thing is going to be decided by one of us outthinking the other, plain and simple. Now, if you can pick up some money helping me in that, what's the matter with it?"

He saw her hesitate then, and he added, "Besides, Brad doesn't care about Spanish Spur, anyhow. It isn't as though you'd be working against him. Now, how about it?"

She stood looking at him a long moment, and then she said, "All right, but I'm not doing this for nothing."

"Good! Let me know the minute you hear anything worthwhile. You can send that Mex of yours to the hotel. If I'm not there, some of my men will be."

She merely nodded, and he picked up his hat and went out of the room, Lily accompanying him to the door. As he stepped out upon the porch he turned and looked at her a long moment before he murmured wonderingly, "Is there anything besides ice water in your veins, Lily?"

She said, "Penn, clever speech is really not in your line." And closed the door.

The wagon had mired down on the approaches to Buffalo Creek, and, in extricating it, the team had split the doubletree, necessitating Embree's riding three miles to the nearest farm to borrow another. Consequently, Embree and Houghton did not reach the Meeker homestead until shortly after the early first darkness. The rain had stopped an hour ago, the air had turned crisp, and overhead an occasional star winked through, indicating clearing weather on the morrow.

From some distance up the Valley, they had seen lights near the house, and as they turned into the yard a man hailed them and advanced, holding a lantern aloft. Houghton replied, and then Embree recognized the thin leathery features of Sim Darby. A dozen others now moved out of the shadows toward the wagon, and Embree caught the glint of lantern light on a shotgun barrel. Another lantern flared, shedding its bright pattern over the grim faces of the farmers.

Then they were lifting Meeker's body from the wagon and carrying it to the house. As the door opened, Embree caught a glimpse of the shack's shabby interior: the rude furniture, the puncheon floor, and the bleak faces of farm women; he saw the frightened eyes of a young girl who stared at the burden they were bringing in, clapped her hand to her mouth, and turned into a neighbor woman's comforting arms. It was deathly still. Then the door closed.

Darby and some of the others had waited near Embree, who still sat the saddle. Tom Houghton climbed down over the wheel and came to join them. In the lantern's light Darby's face showed a bitter suspicion as he turned to Embree and said, "Seems funny that a cowman would do what you did in town. And what are you doin' down here?"

"Isn't it plain enough?" Embree asked, surprised.

Houghton wheeled toward Darby with a low exclamation of disgust. "He saved my life, Sim. And he helped me get Meeker out of there. I don't thank you for taking that tone."

"Sure! We're all obliged," a farmer back in the crowd growled sarcastically. "Can we also thank him for Drummond's movin' in against us already?"

"Now, what's this?" Embree murmured.

Darby kept looking at him steadily. "Not over an hour ago Bob Hackett and a crew rode through here and practically ordered us off our land—sell to Drummond or take the consequences." He hesitated, then blurted bitterly, "That's what crossin' Drummond gets you!"

"Would it be any different if you lay down in the mud before him?" Embree drawled.

Darby made a gesture but had no immediate reply, and Embree said dryly, "It's your land. Every man set his own price on his property."

"That's easy to say when you got none!" a man snapped, with resentful finality, and when there was no reply they turned as by a single accord and went to the house.

Embree accepted this with a grim resignation, sympathizing with them, yet knowing that they had no monopoly on the coming trouble. He stared into the darkness as they left, hearing Houghton, beside him, mutter angrily, "The fools! The blasted fools!"

"Never mind, Tom," Embree said. "Come here a minute."

As the farmer approached and halted, Embree fished some bills from his pocket, peeled two of them from the small wad, and handed these to Houghton. He said, "You slip this to Meeker's widow, and just forget where it came from."

Houghton was still a moment, then he took the money and looked up at Embree, saying in a low voice,

"They need this, bad. And, Embree, you're one fine gent."

"It doesn't call for a medal," Embree said, with mild reproof. "Those kids had to be hungry for Meeker to butcher somebody else's beef." With that, he booted his horse on into the northward way, calling, "Just forget the whole thing."

He was still mulling over the disturbing news of Drummond's move against the farmers when, much later, he rounded into the yard of Spanish Spur. The lights were on in both the big house and the bunkhouse, and in their faint reflection he saw two horses hitched by the corral. He was unsaddling as the door of the bunkhouse opened and Tal Evans came over the yard toward him.

"Well, the prodigal son has returned," Evans observed laconically, taking the bridle from Embree's hand. "There's a family conference."

Embree was ready with a reply but did not give it, for at that moment they both heard the oncoming, laboring run of a horse; he waited, turning toward the sound, and sound and rider came on rapidly, reached them, and stopped. The rider's shape leaned forward in the saddle and he called, "Embree?"

"It's me, Chuck," he said, and approached the rider, one of the hands from the War Bow Valley line camp. "What's the trouble?"

"I think we're in for it," Chuck said, a subdued excitement in his voice. "This afternoon that Taos fellow brought a crew out to the Valley and made a gather—picked up our beef along with theirs. When me and Wiley rode over to ask how come, he got downright inhospitable. Said if we wanted our cows, to try and get 'em."

The suddenness of it held Embree's closest consideration for a long moment; he stood very still staring into the darkness, thinking that this was of the same pattern as the abrupt move Drummond had made against the nesters. Then he turned and said calmly, "All right, Chuck—thanks. Put up your horse and get some grub. We'll talk in the morning." He left them, went directly to the house, and rapped on the door.

Amy and Brad sat near the fireplace talking with their father, and as Embree went in to Cal Sutton's summons, he met Brad's sullen defiant stare first, then took off his hat to Amy and went to stand by the fireplace, while Sutton's searching glance rested momentarily upon his face.

"You went down the Valley with Meeker's body?"

Embree looked swiftly from him to Amy, and Sutton explained, "Arnim gave us the whole story."

"I went with Houghton," Embree then said.

"You did the right thing. It's long past time that somebody faced Drummond down, and I'm glad it was Spanish Spur that did it."

Embree's dark eyes lighted briefly with appreciation, and then he pulled his long lips into a thin grimace and said laconically, "I don't think Drummond appreciated it." He saw their attention quicken, and told them what he had learned down at Meeker's place, and of the tidings that Chuck had just brought in from War Bow Valley.

"The farmers seemed to think I'd made a mistake," he concluded, with grave candor. "Maybe so, for it's plain that Drummond means to move smack into this thing now. He'll try to run the nesters out of the country, and of course that gather down in the Valley is just to test us out, to see if we take him up." He waited.

Cal Sutton was staring into the fire as Embree finished, his face hard, his mouth drawn tight. After a brief span he nodded, saying in an oddly calm voice, "Just so. There comes a time when a man has to stand up to whatever's facing him, and I think we've reached that place. Drummond will get his fight."

Amy and Brad were staring at him in some surprise; after a moment, Brad said, "Why, that's ridiculous! He wouldn't want to start an open war, and if he did, what could we do?"

Cal Sutton raised his head, looked straight at his son a moment, and said scornfully, "The law of any range is that a man can cut for his own cows. Tomorrow we'll go down and cut that herd." He turned to Embree. "See to it that the crew is ready in the morning."

Embree nodded, saying nothing, his face showing a small embarrassment for Cal Sutton. Amy, who had heard all this with a deep uneasy concern, was watching how the light laid bare the strong dark planes of Embree's face, how it glistened in his jet-black hair; even the cutting penetration of his gaze at this moment seemed to give him a tough bladelike quality, and she told herself, That's what he wanted—and I'm glad he did. Then a worry rose up in her, and she turned to her father.

"Dad, won't Drummond have his gunmen there?"

"Very likely. But where could a man go and not meet them from now on?"

She watched Embree as this reply was given, and saw no change in his face; he looked at her briefly, the dark eyes probing hers for an instant, and then he turned away. But in that instant she read all the stubborn, unbeaten qualities of the man, and she was both glad and oddly apprehensive.

Out of the silence that had settled, Cal Sutton said, "You can't do anything here, Amy. Better start back to town before it gets too late. Brad will go with you."

Brad rose with alacrity, and then Amy got up wordlessly and began putting on her things. There was a silence in the room, the intangible feeling that a point had been reached beyond which a pattern familiar to them all would no longer reach.

Brad was tramping across the porch to bring up the horses. Amy kissed her father good night and straightened, looking at Embree. "I think that you did a good thing in town, no matter what comes of it," she said. "But you'll have to be careful from now on."

It seemed to him that there was a tenderness in her voice and in her regard that he had never before seen, and for just a moment he felt the warm pleasant shock of it. Then she went out, he heard her walk across the porch, and afterward he heard the horses make their small commotion of departure. Telling himself that he had imagined it, he turned to find the rancher watching him steadily.

"I'm riding down there with you tomorrow," Sutton said quietly.

They looked straight at each other for a moment then. Embree could have said a lot of things: that Sutton was too ill; that he could handle it himself; that it wasn't necessary. But Cal Sutton's eyes were telling him imperatively that none of these would be the right answer. Presently he said softly, "Cal, there's some sicknesses that no doctor can prescribe for. I don't blame you."

With a nod, he crossed the room to the corridor leading to his office in a wing of the house. As he went, Sutton was again staring steadily into the flames.

Brad Sutton left Amy at the house in town and rode on to the back street, where he dismounted before Lily Farnum's house, went up the walk, and rapped on the door. As Lily opened, he stepped inside, then stopped, his hands on her arms, and regarded her hungrily a moment before he kissed her. After a while she pushed away, looking up at him with a small smile.

"Aren't you coming in, Brad?"

He shook his head. "I can't stay, and I'd give my right arm if I could." He kept looking at her, and then, moved by the sight of her, he once more drew her to him, holding her close. "Ah, Lily," he muttered wretchedly, "a man should never love a woman the way I love you—he's no longer his own man when he does."

She cocked her head back, her eyes searching his face. She said in a low tone, "Why! You really mean it, don't you?"

"Have you ever doubted it?"

"Then why must you go?"

Brad made a gesture of disgust. "Penn Drummond rounded up some of our beef along with his down in War Bow Valley, and he's daring us to come and get it." He laughed shortly. "The old man's snorting and pawing the ground, and I guess we'll have to go down tomorrow and get it back."

"I see." Lily drew a little farther back from him, her eyes changing slightly. "Does this mean that you people are going to fight Drummond?"

"How could we?" Brad said, with light scorn. "No, this is just a question of cutting the herd. Who wants to fight? Not me! In fact there's only one thing I want, and you know what it is."

"Tell me," she said, in a low thick voice.

He shook his head with a heavy hopelessness, saying with almost tragic misery, "I'd be the happiest man in the world if you'd marry me and let me get you out of this place. The hope of that keeps me going, Lily."

All at once, she found it difficult to meet his gaze, and she turned away, murmuring in a low tone, "You—you shouldn't say that, Brad. It's no use."

"Ah," he chided, "are you always going to dance away from me like this? It is no game to me, Lily. Surely you can see that!"

"Please!"

He made a gesture of resignation and stepped back, and at that she turned. "Not now, Brad—just not now. Later. I—perhaps you'd better go. And please—be careful."

When he had gone, Lily Farnum stood with her back to the door, hearing his retreating footsteps, staring at nothing. Then she went slowly to the living room and rang a small bell on the sideboard. Presently an aged Mexican came from the rear of the house.

"*A su mandar, mi señora.*"

She hesitated only a moment, then said, "Juan, go to Mr. Drummond at the hotel. Tell him that Sutton is sending his men to War Bow Valley tomorrow to cut the herd of cattle that Drummond's men are holding there. *Entiendes bien?*"

"*Como no, Señora?*" Juan murmured. "I go directly."

When he had gone, Lily sank into a chair. After a while she murmured half aloud, "You must not fall in love with him, Lily Farnum—it would ruin everything. And remember—you had that once, and what did it bring you?"

Embree was up and dressed as the sun of the first clear day in weeks touched the tips of the Bowstrings with a pink aura. At breakfast he told the crew what lay ahead of them, and they took the news without enthusiasm. Although they would pick up three more riders on the way to the Valley, every man there knew that they would be outnumbered if it came to a fight.

They were saddling up when Cal Sutton and Brad came from the house, and all but Embree stared in surprise at Sutton as he came down the steps, disdaining Brad's help. Only the stiff whiteness about Sutton's lips and the mechanical slowness of his movements betrayed the pain which this effort was costing him.

Brad went for his horse, and Embree held the bridle of Sutton's gray gelding as Sutton, with a suppressed groan, pulled himself up into the leather. When they were all aboard, Sutton turned to Embree. "You give them the story, Jim?"

"They know."

"Then let's ride." Sutton booted his horse forward, Embree moved up to his side, and the others fell in behind.

They rode up into the first rises of the Medicines, then followed the southward thrust of the hills. The weather had taken a definite turn: jays shrilled and flashed through the trees, smaller birds chittered, and the smell of spring's bursting freshness closed them in as the sun rose over the peaks of the Bowstrings eastward and touched the damp earth, the grass, the leaves.

An hour after leaving the ranch, they came to the two hundred cattle. They hit the valley floor and rode down the outslope into War Bow Valley. The herd lay a mile north of the old Post, near a finger of timber reaching out into the grass from the hills. A chuck wagon was near the woods, and beyond the wagon a half dozen riders tightly herded a gather of perhaps two hundred cattle. They hit the valley floor and rode directly toward the camp.

Drummond's men had seen them now, and the guard began pulling slowly away from the cattle—a fact which Embree noted with a small tightening of the stomach.

They kept on, bunched up a little, and when they were forty yards from the wagon, three riders reined out from behind it, rode forward a way, and stopped, indolently cupping their hands on the horn as they waited. It came to Embree then that by that action a balance had already been tipped against Spanish Spur.

Thirty feet or so separated Sutton from the D Slash men when he threw up his hand and halted.

Taos, Drummond's still-faced gunman, sat his horse between the other two riders, and now Sutton looked straight at him a moment, shifted his weight in the saddle, and cast a slow glance around, seeming to sense uneasily something hidden here. Embree had felt the same thing: it was something in the wind; it was on the faces of the men before them.

Taos said insolently, "You're too late for breakfast, and dinner's not till noon. I can't ask you to get down, Sutton."

His arrogance rubbed Cal Sutton against a grain that was already pretty raw. He flushed, his eyes narrowing, but said calmly enough, "Never mind. We just came to cut this herd."

"That's too bad," Taos said lazily. "You can't cut it—not now."

Embree spoke up. "We'll just ride through, quiet, and see if there's any Spanish Spur stuff. If not, no harm done. If there is——"

"You won't cut at all," Taos said softly. "This is trail stuff, and we don't want it choused around. If any of your stuff's here, we'll cut it back later."

Instantly there was a wall here, thrown up in their faces. It could not be talked around, and a man could not back away from it and live on in this country. It was all very clear to every soul. The raw uncaring arrogance of it pushed Cal Sutton over the margin of his judgment: he was tired of losing, dog-weary of weighing and reweighing threats, and he would have no more of it.

His face turned a swift angry purple, and he stiffened in his stirrups. "You damned gunslick!" he shouted at Taos. "You've got my cows in that herd, and we're going to cut. You can have it peaceful, or you can have it——"

Then Taos clawed at his gun. Even before it cleared the leather, the long angry whine of a bullet went over their heads and a rifle shot rapped out from the timber. A man yelped, frightened, "Ambush! They got us whipsawed!" and as the horses went into a nervous skittering, the fire burst up with sultry violence, and Embree jerked his gun up out of the holster.

CHAPTER FOUR

EMBREE SAW Taos swing his horse about and aim directly at him. In the fraction of a second that this impression lasted, he spurred his animal, and it leaped just as Taos' gun crashed. The bullet breathed by Embree, and he fired at Taos and saw him leap out of the saddle, then lay his gun over the pommel.

These things happened almost as one, and now the angry bee-sing of lead was coming at them from the timber, and a pair of guns concealed in the wagon had joined in. Cal Sutton's gun was booming wrathily, and all at once Sutton lifted his shout over the firing, "Cut 'em down! Show 'em who runs this range!" The others were firing ineffectually as they tried to control their skittering horses.

Embree was a moving target before Taos' sights, and Taos' horse was jerking wild-eyed at the reins. A burst came across the saddle at Embree, but wide of its mark; he heard Cal Sutton grunt, then give a shallow cough, and Taos' horse leaped away and Embree shot as the gunman went at a low crouching run toward the wagon. He saw Taos stumble and fall, roll over and then start crawling, only to collapse. Embree wheeled around then just as Cal Sutton bent toward the ground, falling from the saddle, and Embree grabbed the bridle of Sutton's gray and held the rancher on the leather.

At the same moment he caught the quick frightened look on Wiley's countenance and saw Brad Sutton, whitefaced, firing wildly into the timber. In one dreary flash, Embree knew that this was a water haul, and possibly a catastrophe; and every man there knew it, too.

Suddenly Tal Evans shouted above the racket, "We came for cattle—not for a fight. Let's go!" Without waiting for an answer he spurred away, and another followed him, and another. Embree, holding Sutton's limp weight against his shoulder, barked out, "Pull out, Spanish Spur—it's no dice!" and with that the other riders broke off the fight so suddenly as to be almost startling, wheeled their horses, and galloped out of range.

Embree had managed to get his horse and Sutton's turned away. Brad had now seen what was happening, and he spurred in close to lend a hand, his face a startled gray. As he did so, a wicked shout came from over near the wagon: "Get that damned Texan!" and then two guns roared as one and Embree heard the slugs thud into Cal Sutton. There was no reaction in Sutton's body, and he knew then that Sutton had been dead even before they hit him.

As they pulled away out of range, the firing stopped. Sutton was slumped over the horn, supported between Embree and Brad, and blood stained the saddle and smeared the skirts of his rig crimson. Brad was swearing softly, an incredulous anger on his face. They stopped where the other riders had pulled up, Embree dismounted and gently eased Cal Sutton's body to the ground, and a moment later Brad joined him as he bent over the rancher.

Cal Sutton was dead, the front of his shirt red-stained by three separate bullet holes. Embree, looking down at him, was thinking grimly of that cry from the wagon: those last two shots had been meant for him, not Sutton, and a strange pity for the dead man who had shielded him hit him squarely in the chest.

The hands were staring glumly at their dead boss. Presently one of them said, softly querulous, "Damn it all, it was like they knowed we was comin'. They had it all set."

"Sure they did," Tal Evans agreed. "You don't set a trap unless you expect to catch something, do you?"

Chuck said, "That's certain. Last night when me and Wiley rode into their camp, there was only four—five of 'em. The others came in later. Then they hid those guns in the timber and in the wagon this morning. They expected us."

"But how could they?" Brad Sutton asked in a strained voice, straightening. His face was dead white, and a shocked unbelief lay in his eyes.

Chuck shrugged. For a moment no one spoke, until Brad said almost hopefully, "They could've just figured we'd move this way—outguessed us—couldn't they?"

Embree had said nothing in this time, but now he pushed up from his hunkers and looked at Brad levelly, his face almost expressionless. "They could have, but they didn't," he said quietly. "The only thing they didn't know was that your father would come with us." And then he motioned to a couple of the riders.

They tied Cal Sutton's body over the saddle and rode in gloomy silence out of the Valley. Just as they came to the rise of the Medicine Hills, Embree turned in the saddle and looked back. A good dozen men were congregated about the wagon, and the herd was scattering. They had never, he knew, intended to put that beef on the trail. It had been a decoy in a plan laid to get him, Embree; but perhaps it had worked out even better for Drummond, for Spanish Spur was now without Cal Sutton to head it. After a little while, thinking of that, Embree saw it differently: Cal Sutton was dead because of him. A heaviness settled over him, and as they rode on he had the odd thought, this is the first day of that sunshine that Cal was praying for for the past month.

The funeral was to be held from the Methodist Church in town, in whose small burial plot Cal Sutton's wife had been interred these many years. As Jim Embree rode through the late morning sunshine into Wells, past the small white-painted church with its arched stained-glass windows, he saw the freshly turned mound of earth in the grassy quadrangle behind the church and knew once more the baffled anger—almost a personal hurt—that Cal Sutton's death had caused him.

There was a casual uncaring pointlessness about Sutton's killing that shocked him. In two years of working for Sutton, Embree had begun by admiring his courage in the face of adversity and had ended by having for him a quiet affection that was anchored upon the man's human qualities. Sutton had firmly believed that the farmers of War Bow Valley could live side by side with the cattlemen—a rare enough trait; his compassion for the unfortunates among the hoemen had more than once caused him to close his eyes to a slaughtered beef, to a green hide on a nester's corral fence. His was a kindliness that would be missed.

Recalling these things, Embree felt a renewal of the helpless bitter anger that had hardened him yesterday when, bringing the news of her father's death to Amy, he had viewed her stunned bewilderment, her dry-eyed grief. The memory of that did him no good, and he tried to push it from his mind and could not.

It lacked a few minutes of noon as Embree rounded in at the rack before the courthouse. His preoccupation slipped away from him as he glanced through the street, noting the large number of nesters' wagons lining the margins of the street's lower end; he saw the unusual sight of farmers walking the streets in clean shirts and Sunday best suits on this, a weekday, and momentarily he pondered this phenomenon; then he moved over the boardwalk to the sheriff's office in a wing of the courthouse.

Sheriff Carl Odlum looked up as Embree entered, a faint irritation fleeting through his pale gray eyes before he lifted his feet off the desk and let them thud down to the floor. "Embree," he murmured, not warmly. "Take a chair."

Embree chose to remain standing. Fishing his pipe from his pocket, he tamped down the half-smoked load and lit it, pulling the fire slowly into the bowl; afterward he looked up and asked casually, "Any luck on the man who killed Meeker, Carl?"

"No." Odlum watched Embree carefully a moment, adding in a paper-dry voice, "Everybody was in the street. Who'd have seen him?"

"And who'd tell if he did?" Odlum's face clouded, and Embree added laconically, "Too bad you weren't in town that day, Carl. But I suppose that business over at Three Forks couldn't be helped."

"You can suppose anything you want to. As for arresting anybody, where would a man start?"

"You really want to know?"

Odlum studied the question, suspicious of it, thinking fast. "Are you trying to tell me how to run my office, Embree?"

Because Embree respected human life, the wanton waste of it revolted him. He had known that Odlum, who was Drummond's man, would move slowly, if at all; yet as he observed the man's resentful hedging, Embree's mood grew steadily more truculent, and Odlum's present question was too much.

"Stop it, Odlum!" he said disgustedly. "We both know who had Meeker killed: Penn Drummond."

Odlum started his denial, then clamped his lips shut; he gave Embree a bitter glance, looked away, and said without conviction, "You fool! He was in the street—in plain sight."

"Certainly—with D Slash men laying bets that Meeker would never go back down the Valley alive. Isn't that enough for an investigation?"

Odlum swung his head around, the sharp hard glitter of vexation in his eyes. He stared at Embree a moment, then got up and said, lamely defensive, "When the devil did you become a farmer-lover?"

"Two men killed in two days," Embree reminded him softly. "Are you going to Cal Sutton's funeral?"

The resentment left Odlum's face, and he stood grave and indrawn, like a man empty of words, before he muttered, "That fight was out of my jurisdiction—on federal property."

"Very convenient," said Embree.

Odlum drew a long sigh, unhappy and not liking the taste of shame, but not finding the right response to this goading. "Even if I had jurisdiction, I'd have to pull the whole bunch in," he said wearily. "You along with the rest of them. Don't forget, Drummond had a man nicked, too."

"Give Drummond my sympathy when you see him," Embree drawled.

Odlum flushed hotly and made a move forward, but Embree stepped to meet him, placed his hand on the man's chest, and pushed him backward three paces.

"Be careful, Odlum," he said thinly. "Don't tempt me."

A wild kind of desperation came up in Odlum's eyes at that; he was a man hollowed out, incapable of thought or action, yet needing both; and then his pride revolted, and he threw Embree's hand off and blurted, "Get to hell out of here—and don't come back!"

Embree gave him a curious mild look, turned his back, and went to the door, where he swung around. "Why would I come back here? Penn Drummond's the law in this country."

He left, going directly to the hotel where, at the dining room's arched entrance, he encountered Juston Larribee, Cal Sutton's attorney, who was just departing. Embree halted and they exchanged greetings, and then the lawyer observed, "I understand the services are at two."

"That's right."

Larribee paused for a thoughtful moment. "I was just down at the house, paying my respects, and I told Amy and Brad to come to my office right after the burial for the reading of the will. It may look like hurrying it a. little, but I believe it's important enough to do so." Then he glanced sharply at Embree. "Could you come, too?"

"If you think I ought to."

"I believe you should be present," the lawyer said quietly.

"Then I'll come."

Without further explanation Larribee inclined his head and went on past, and Embree moved into the dining room's midday hubbub, noting again the presence of a number of farmers. Across the room he caught the eye of Sam Arnim, who sat at a table with Moorehead and Jennings and a couple of other small ranchers; he nodded to them and made his way to an empty corner table.

He ordered, and when his meal came he ate abstractedly. Larribee's strange request was puzzling him, for his personal interest in the welfare of Spanish Spur might now be without point; since Cal Sutton's death he had no idea where he stood, no clear picture of the ranch's future.

He was still reflecting upon this as Sam Arnim approached his table, greeted him, and sank into a chair across from him. He saw immediately that some dark thought lay in Arnim's mind and was not surprised when the other said, "I've something I wanted to say: now that Cal is dead, I've got more than an ordinary interest in Spanish Spur, because of Amy. I'll be looking out for her welfare, Embree."

"Why, that's fine," said Embree, keeping his eyes on his plate.

There was a small silence. "The point is," Arnim said, in a stiffer tone, "that all this about Cal comes back to what I told you the other day. Drummond shouldn't have been stirred up. It wasn't necessary."

Embree's sharp gaze rose to Arnim's face. "Cal seemed to think it was," he said quietly.

"I wonder."

"I suppose you think, as usual, that Drummond was right," Embree said caustically. He saw Arnim start to speak, but he went on, "Cal was right in asking for a cut. Drummond forced him into a fight that no self-respecting man could have passed up."

"You're wasting your breath on me with that kind of talk," Arnim said curtly. "I think you pushed Cal into it."

Slowly, Embree shoved his plate aside. His eyes grew chilly as he looked straight at Arnim and said, "If you stand up for Drummond all the time just to rub me the wrong way, you're playing it exactly right, because I'm sick of him. I'm also getting a bellyful of the people who defend him, including you. Now, does that make you feel better, Sam?"

"See here, now—" Arnim began.

But Embree pushed back his chair and rose, stopping Arnim's word with a gesture. He stood looking down at the man a long moment, then said softly, "On the other hand, you've always wanted to hate me and never had a good reason, and maybe that's why. If it is, it may help you to know that I feel the same way about you."

For a long, strained moment their glances held, and then Arnim smiled a thin starved smile. "No, Embree," he said pointedly, with a slow shake of his head. "You don't really hate me— you *just envy* me."

Something in Arnim's eyes challenged him to deny that, and he had the brief impulse to do so; instead, he said quietly, "Now that you mention it, maybe I do." And turning on his heel, he went out.

The small church was crowded. Embree, standing near the door during the brief services, found deeply interesting the presence here of so many farmers from War Bow Valley. From his vantage point he could see Amy up near the front, her small fine profile turned toward him, her cheeks pale and drawn, and the window-filtered sunlight turning her tawny hair into a shimmering golden corona. He studied her for a long moment; and afterward, slowly, the sober weather-scruffed faces of the hoemen, and he did not miss the significance of their presence: they, too, had suffered at Drummond's hands; they, too, had known Cal Sutton as a kindly and charitable man. As the preacher's solemn words droned on, it came to Embree that here, if anywhere, lay an answer, for the farmers as of now stood with Spanish Spur.

The words of a final prayer died away, and after a brief quiet there was a faint stirring through the place. Embree turned and went slowly out into the yard, already taking a new sight on the problem. The church was emptying, and he saw Brad and Amy come out and go around to the graveyard. Without fully knowing why, he did not want to see Cal Sutton put in the ground, and he sighed and walked over to join a group of cowmen who stood quietly conversing at the margin of the yard.

For a time they spoke in sober hushed voices. After a while the crowd began drifting around the church, on the way to horses and wagons. Observing this, Stacey Jennings remarked, "Say what you will, it was decent of these farmers to come to Cal's funeral."

"Or foolish," Moorehead challenged grumpily. "Drummond's not likely to overlook this." He shook his head. "I tell you, the trouble in this country hasn't even begun yet."

Embree stared beyond the man, at the green folds of the Medicines flowing along the horizon. His eyes were almost shut, and daylight danced in them, giving them a diamond sharpness. The sun's heat came down full in the yard and glinted on the panes of the church window, and the air was full of a body of smells: grass, dust, flowers somewhere—and freshly turned earth.

"Now there's an idea," he said softly, turning to Moorehead. "You think the farmers ought to have got permission from Drummond to come to the funeral?"

They all looked at him in surprise, but he left them and walked over to pass a few words with Houghton, who was conversing with a bunch of farmers. As Embree came up the farmers nodded and drifted away. Embree watched them go, saying presently to Houghton, "Quite a few up from the Valley."

"Trouble draws all kinds together," Houghton replied.

"It ought to—in there in the church, I thought of that myself."

Houghton faced about, regarding him keenly. Then he looked away, saying in a quiet voice, "Don't question me about it right now, but if you'll drop down to my place around eight tomorrow night, you may hear something of interest. Jennings will be there, and if you know any other cattlemen you can trust, bring them along." Then he went toward his horse.

Accompanied by Brad and Sam Arnim, Amy was coming across the churchyard. Embree drifted forward, touched his hat, and said, "Larribee asked me to come up to his office for the reading of the will——"

"Couldn't you at least wait till they've filled in the grave?" Arnim growled angrily, glaring at Embree.

A hot flush rose to Embree's cheeks, but Amy said quickly, "Sam, it's all right! Juston wanted us there immediately after the services." Then she turned to Embree. "I'm glad he asked you. We're going straight there."

"Then I'll walk that far with you, Amy," Arnim said instantly, watching Embree.

"Well, all right," Amy agreed. "We can all go together."

There had always been something inside Arnim's head that Embree had never quite reached; but now, after this and after their meeting at the hotel, he knew what it was. He said to Amy, ignoring Arnim, "I've something to do first. I'll see you there."

He rode down the street, slowly considering the thing that he'd found at last in Arnim: the man was jealous of him. It explained much; and then he found himself wondering how he had ever given Arnim cause for feeling that way. Still, he was right—you do envy him because of Amy, he told himself. And yet the admission changed nothing in him that he could see. A man might envy another for many things: a good horse, or a million dollars, or just plain peace of mind. Arnim was a fool, because he, Embree, had no dreams for Amy and himself and never had any. The only thing that this did was deepen a little his already profound dislike of Sam Arnim.

He stood with his lean shoulders against a dusty case of law books while the flat monotony of Larribee's voice droned on. He was seeing Amy's face, her slim full form, through narrowed lids; he was noting Amy's hurt blue eyes which held the distance beyond Larribee's window, and he was thinking with an odd wonder of the keenness of Sam Arnim's perception....

Abruptly the lawyer stopped reading and cleared his throat. "Perhaps I'd better repeat that section?" and Amy jerked her attention back to him, saying, "I—I'm sorry, Juston. Please do."

Larribee gazed with brief reproach over the rims of his spectacles, then intoned, "Section Eight. It is my further will that said ranch property be held jointly by my son, Bradley Sutton, and my daughter, Amy Sutton; that that portion thereof north of Buffalo Creek and extending to the line adjacent to the Medicine Hills and containing the house and fixtures shall be the share of Amy Sutton, while that from Buffalo Creek southward shall be the share of Bradley Sutton, who always shall have the right of domicile in the ranch house; and, furthermore, that the aforesaid Bradley and Amy Sutton shall manage their separate shares as one, consulting freely with each other on matters of mutual interest; and in the event of the death of either, his/her share shall revert to the surviving heir, provided that he or she leaves neither spouse nor issue."

Larribee stopped reading and slowly laid the document on the desk, afterward removing his glasses and wiping them thoughtfully with his handkerchief. There was silence in the office, broken at last by Amy, who said hesitantly, "I—I'm not sure that I understand, Juston. Does that mean that the ranch is a partnership?"

Larribee pursed his lips, shaking his head. "No-o-o," he said, "not exactly, Amy. It is not a legal partnership, but rather a moral one. It was your father's intention that you would conduct it so, working closely together all the time, but legally free of one another."

"I see." Amy turned to look at Brad, who smiled and spread his hands. She seemed to have something to say about this, but after a moment she rose, saying merely, "Thank you, Juston. You've been very kind."

"You both have my deepest sympathy," Larribee said sincerely. "And—I'm sure that this arrangement will work out all right."

"Of course it will," she replied earnestly.

Brad rose, agreeing, "There's no reason why it shouldn't."

Embree then was meeting Larribee's straight stare, catching a look in it that he could not interpret; a moment later, he stepped out into the hall, holding the door open for Amy. As he did so, a man's figure scuttled into the stair well and disappeared. Instinctively, Embree started to pursue, then checked himself. The sound of boots was hitting rapidly down the stairs, and he was aware that whoever the eavesdropper had been, he would soon be lost in the street.

Amy and Brad had come out behind him, and Amy now asked, "What was that?"

Embree shrugged. "Sounded like someone going down nearly fell on the stairs."

She raised a dubious eyebrow, then walked on with Brad, and Embree, following, was at the head of the stairs when Larribee called, "Embree, can I see you a moment?"

Telling Amy that he would be along to the house later, Embree returned to Larribee's office. The lawyer was staring pensively down at the pages of Cal Sutton's will, and as Embree entered he looked up, observing dryly, "Now you may see why I wanted you here."

"It seems an odd arrangement."

The lawyer nodded thoughtfully. "Cal Sutton was a strange man in many ways," he said slowly, "and a smart man, too. In this case—well, I'm not so sure. I advised him against this plan, of course, but he would have it no other way."

"Then he must have had good reasons," Embree said.

"The best, as reasons go. More than anything else, he wanted Spanish Spur to go on after his death, but he felt that even that wouldn't be worth while unless it did so through the good will and the mutual desire of his children." Larribee had been looking down at the desk, and now he raised his eyes slowly to Embree's. "He believed that this arrangement would hold the ranch together, and, moreover, bring his children together and help to straighten Brad out by placing a little responsibility on his shoulders." He paused, regarding Embree, then asked, "What's your opinion?"

Embree shrugged. "It's a poor time to experiment, but a man's will is his will."

"Exactly," said Larribee. "Amy is solid, but Brad is the question mark. That's what I wanted to speak to you about—so that you would keep it in mind."

"But why me? Brad is his own man, Juston."

"No, he's not," the lawyer said firmly. "Where this will is concerned, there is an obligation on him. Oh, I'll admit that maybe the will isn't good law, but it's excellent human sentiment, which is more important." He stopped, and then said deliberately, "It's going to be up to you to see that Cal Sutton's faith was justified, Embree."

Their glances held, and presently Embree said, "Juston, I may not even have a job. Cal Sutton hired me, and he's dead."

"Nonsense, man! You've got a bigger job than ever."

But there were too many unknown factors yet for Embree to make a commitment at this moment, and after an interval he said slowly, "We'll see, Juston. In the meantime, thanks for telling me this."

He left and went downstairs, where he paused a moment in the doorway, his sharp glance running the street. Up the way, a group of Drummond's men stood before the saloon, and among them he recognized Taos, wearing a bandage under his crumpled black Stetson, and what Odlum had told him about one of Drummond's men having been nicked came back to him.

As he stepped down to the boardwalk, they saw him and broke off their talk. Embree waited, watching them, but they made no move and presently he showed them his back and cruised unhurriedly down toward Amy's house, As he went, Larribee's words lingered in his mind, setting up a conflict in him; he had been given a job whose accomplishment was opposed by every force at work in this strange situation with possibly the exception of Amy. He was not even certain that he wanted to do it himself. And then he remembered how Cal Sutton had died, the deep sense of gratitude came back, and he thought, see what Amy says about it.

CHAPTER FIVE

A MY SAT on the horsehair sofa in the living room, her hands folded in her lap, her blue eyes seeming a deeper blue because of some inner preoccupation, as she looked at Embree who leaned his tall frame against the mantelpiece and pulled slowly on his pipe.

"I wanted to get your idea about something," she said slowly, almost as though choosing her words. "It's a rather odd arrangement between Brad and me, and I was wondering—can either of us do as we please with our share? Legally, I mean?"

He considered that slowly, then nodded. "I believe you can."

For a moment longer she regarded him, before murmuring, "I see. The reason I asked is that Sam Arnim just made me an offer for my share of Spanish Spur."

Embree's glance sharpened. "Arnim? But how did he——?"

"He was outside Larribee's office," Amy explained. "I saw no reason for his not knowing about the will, so I told him." She paused, looking down at her clasped hands, then added in a reflective tone, "He seems pretty certain that Drummond will get War Bow Valley and force Spanish Spur into a corner. And then—" she shrugged—"we'll have to take what we can settle for." All at once she raised her eyes, full and wide, to Embree. "Tell me, what do you think?"

He really was thinking that one day when Amy married Sam Arnim, her share of Spanish Spur would go to Box A anyhow; that was the logic of it, but he felt a deep resentment at this move of Arnim's. It was true that Amy stood unprotected, now that the ranch had been divided and Drummond was on the move and Cal Sutton was no longer here to face him. Still, Arnim was taking a lot for granted.

He said carefully, feeling her out, "There may be something to what Arnim says. And if you sold, at least you wouldn't have to teach school any longer."

"That's so." She was watching him oddly. "But suppose I did sell. What would you do?"

"You needn't worry about me," he assured her, with a shake of the head. "I've been thinking for some time of going in with a friend on a horse ranch down near Alamogordo."

He turned away a little, not seeing the numbed lost look that came into Amy's eyes as she glanced down and smoothed her skirt over her knees. He heard her say, "I see. Well, I don't blame you. Perhaps there's a beating at the end of this anyway, and I suppose I have no right to ask anyone to take on such a job. Now that Dad's gone, it can only mean trouble of the worst kind."

She had voiced this in a tone of reluctant hopelessness that brought him around, looking at her intently. She still sat staring down at her hands, and he hesitated, puzzled by word and tone, before he spoke.

"But I thought you wanted to sell."

At once, she lifted her head and looked straight at him. "But I don't. I want to keep Spanish Spur together—a going concern."

A strong good feeling came to him then, surprising even himself, and he smiled, the darkness of his face lighting as he said, "I guess we didn't understand each other. To be frank about it, I wasn't sure whether I'd be needed any longer or not."

"But you are! I want you to stay, if you will, Embree." She held herself still, waiting. Embree was watching the glow which was growing up beneath the darker depths of her eyes. It seemed to come out of deep places in her, and it was no mere trick of the sunlight coming in here, but rather an evidence of her spirit, some vestige of what had been Cal Sutton, too.

"Then I'll stay," he said.

The look of hope came fully alive in her eyes, and she rose and came to him. "Thank you, Embree," she said, in a low earnest voice. "I honestly don't know what I'd do if you left."

"I'll be around as long as you need me," he told her. Their glances held, and he felt that strong unsettling awareness of her coming over him, and again he seemed to find in her eyes and in her voice some quality almost of affection for him. Then all at once she turned away and walked across the room and stood looking out the window for a brief interval. When she faced him, her countenance had changed.

"So that's settled," she said. "Now, tell me: what are our chances?"

"There's no use kidding ourselves. Drummond's aim is to get War Bow Valley, and if he does, he could break Spanish Spur, or at least force it back to the hill graze. He won't have any interference from the law, and he's already thrown a scare into everyone who might fight him. It's going to be a tough haul."

She was watching him very soberly. "Do you think we can hold out against him?"

"To tell the plain truth, we'll need luck. If we could stiffen the backs of the farmers, they might help us hold the Valley, but that's doubtful comfort. And, if Drummond gets it, he can cut off the water from half our graze." He lifted his shoulders, let them fall. "Our job will be to do everything possible to keep him from getting War Bow."

She shook her head a little, saying ruefully, "A big job. And I have to pass it all on to you——"

"I'm not complaining. I just want you to see how things are. Brad, too, for that matter," he added pointedly.

Her answer came at him swiftly. "I'll vouch for Brad. We talked on the way here, and he's with me in this."

Embree said nothing, and after a moment Amy moved toward him and stopped, her eyes searching his face briefly before she said, with disconcerting directness, "I have faith in you to do this thing if it can be done at all, and I'll stand back of you and help all I can. My father trusted you, and his judgment is good enough for me." Then, her eyes changing, she added quickly, "I mean to say—it's my judgment, too."

Embree felt a mild touch of embarrassment and showed it, and at that Amy, too, felt a rush of confusion and abruptly held out her hand. "Good night, Embree."

With a slow smile, he took her hand. "I'll do what I can. And—thanks."

"No, it's I who should thank you."

Embree picked his hat off the table and went toward the door. As he went out, Amy smiled at him, and afterward she stood for some moments looking after his tall lean figure as he strode up the street.

From a deep chair in the lobby of the hotel, Penn Drummond moodily surveyed the traffic through the main street of Wells. The muscles of his square jaw were corded, and he held his cigar in a viselike clamp between large square teeth as he watched the nesters moving in wagons and on horseback on their way out of town.

After a while he rose, scowling, and tramped up the stairs to his room, where Hackett and Taos were waiting. As he came in, they looked up, saw his dark frown, and Hackett murmured, "All those farmers in town just for Sutton's funeral?"

Drummond grunted. "The damn place was full of 'em—as thick as bees in clover." He took a turn across the room and back, his hands clenched behind him and his heavy face showing his seething dissatisfaction. It was plain that the farmers had taken this way of showing their defiance of him, and that fact angered him even while it worried him. Suddenly he broke off his pacing and turned to stare at the others.

"It was a mistake to kill Sutton," he said flatly. "Everybody liked him. And now, they've got a point to organize around——"

Taos squared around in his chair, staring at Drummond. "I told you," he said in a deadly quiet tone, "it was the way Embree jerked the horses around. I don't want to hear any more about it."

A harsh reply rose to Drummond's tongue, but he took it out in a hard look at his gunman, saying then, "I'm just trying to add this up : they lose Meeker, and Spanish Spur loses Sutton. That brings 'em together against us." He paused, frowning, and then went on, "If they ever got together, we'd be right on margin——"

"They won't organize," Hackett scoffed. "They've got no guts."

"Don't fool yourself about those farmers. If they had someone to lead them, they'd be pure poison. And Embree or Houghton, either one, could do it."

"Then get rid of those two and quit worrying so much."

"Fine logic," said Drummond disgustedly. "You think a piece of luck will stretch indefinitely? No! There'll be no more gunplay for a while."

"That don't go for Embree," Taos said quietly.

"It goes for anybody." He held Taos' glance, seeming to consider narrowly before he added slowly, "That's not the way. We've got to build up power to match any possible combination of theirs." He turned to regard Hackett. "Bob," he said deliberately, "I think you and I are going to ride up to Long Reach and hire us some men."

"May not be a bad idea," Hackett agreed laconically. "That stock you had the crew push over on Spanish Spur yesterday is dead certain to start some trouble."

"Exactly—and we want to be ready for it, if Amy Sutton decides to see this thing through——"

A rap on the door cut off his speech. Drummond moved toward the door, opened it, and a puncher slipped inside, nodded shortly, and said with sly satisfaction, "Well, I got the dope. No trouble at all—although Embree damn near caught me with my ear to the keyhole."

"All right, all right!" Drumond said impatiently. "What is it?"

"The girl gets everything north of Buffalo Creek, and Brad takes that below. They operate the ranch jointly."

There was stillness in the room as they took the news. Drummond was considering it, looking at it from all sides, and, as he did so, a slow grin began to pull wide his big mouth. He said musingly, "Good work, Stan," and wandered over to the window. For some moments he stood there, the crafty grin settling on his face, and then, all at once, his dark glance sharpened as he saw Lily Farnum strolling down the boardwalk from upstreet.

He left the window, an urgency coming over him as he said shortly to Hackett, "Wait for me, Bob," clapped his hat on his head, and hurried down to the street. On the boardwalk he slowed his pace so as to encounter Lily before the feed store, out of earshot of passers-by. He tipped his hat to her as he came up, muttered a greeting, and took her utterly cool acknowledgment.

Lily was studying Drummond while they made brief small talk, as Drummond recognized and acknowledged by his small sly smile. At last she said abruptly, "All right, Penn. What now?"

"I was just wondering if you'd like to make a thousand dollars."

She was silent for a moment, suspicion in her eyes. Then she murmured, "Naturally. Who wouldn't?"

"Ah, that's the question, isn't it?" Deliberately, Drummond struck a match to his cold cigar and puffed a bright coal into it before he said casually, "I understand Brad Sutton will have control of half of Spanish Spur's range. If you could convince him to give me an option on his share, the thousand would be yours, Lily."

A look of cold anger came into her face. She said, in a low hating voice, "Not for five million. I'm sorry that I listened to you in the first place. There will be no more of it, Drummond."

His gaze sharpened, then became narrow and mean. "Well, well," he mused softly. "Why not?"

"Because you lied to me," she said with icy loathing. "You used the information I sent to you to kill Brad Sutton's father. You made me indirectly the cause of it, and if I were a man I would thrash you within an inch of your dirty life."

He took this with unruffled equanimity, studying her keenly, only a slight tightening about his month betraying his feelings. At last he said gently, "Lily, I have a theory about you: I think you like Brad Sutton a lot. Now, would you want him to know that you sold me the information that resulted in his father's death?"

He saw the fury that darkened her eyes and pulled the blood from her face until it was dead white. She breathed heavily, and a violent anger rose up in her, just to the point of eruption. "You filthy blackmailer!" she said, in a thick unsteady voice. "You wouldn't dare!"

He sighed with mock regret. "Ah, but I'd have to, Lily—unless you get me the option. And don't forget: a thousand dollars can do things for a sick conscience that would surprise you."

She stood pale and rigid for a long moment, hate in her eyes, but he regarded her unperturbed, patient. At last he heard her long sigh, and she moved past him, saying almost inaudibly, "You win, Drummond—and may you scorch in a very special kind of hell!"

CHAPTER SIX

A THIN SPLINTER of light leaking from the margin of a covered window was the only beacon in the darkness as Jim Embree rode into the yard of Houghton's homestead and dismounted. Seeing the black shapes of horses against the lighter darkness at the side of the house, he led his mount that way and tied, and as he turned away, a voice cut sharp and nervous out of the shadows. "Give your name, mister! And remember—you're covered."

"Jim Embree."

The man drifted forward, peering tentatively, then recognized him and said with notable relief, "All right—come along," and they went toward the cabin.

Inside, Embree stood a moment, accustoming his eyes to the pale gold light of the single lamp which burned on the table in the room's center. The still serious faces of a half dozen men about the table, and as many others back in the shadows along the wall, were turned to him. Among them Embree recognized Houghton, Darby, and others; nor was he surprised to see Stacey Jennings there, along with Ernst Mueller, a rancher from Lobo Valley.

The man who had followed Embree in closed and barred the door, then turned to Houghton. "He's the last one, Tom. Get it started."

After nodding to Embree, Houghton glanced around the room, cleared his throat, and began, "You all know why we're here—no use to go into that. But in a nutshell, it means that we're going to lose out to Drummond unless we can get together on some way to fight him." He paused, then added dubiously, "The thing that ain't plain is what we're going to do. Now, let's hear some ideas from you fellows." He sat back and waited.

To Embree, who had remained standing back against the wall, it slowly became apparent that their silence came from some wavering doubt in themselves. He was certain of it when a stringy farmer coughed nervously and said, with apologetic mildness, "Tom, you sure you ain't makin' too much of this? Drummond's not actually botherin' us down here, except by windy threats." He paused, then suggested, "Maybe if we'd just be careful of his cattle and mind our own business..." His voice trailed off, not wholly hopeful.

One or two nodded their heads in agreement, but Houghton said firmly, "You're wrong, Harve. He killed Meeker, didn't he? You all know, too, that he's laid it down that this is going to stay cow country, and we'd find it out. Why do you think he sent his bunch down to 'buy' us out?" He spelled this out for them with a kind of weary patience, and Embree, watching them carefully, saw them accept it reluctantly, saw their deeper wish that it were not true.

After a brief silence, Sim Darby spoke up. "Maybe that's all so, but we ain't fightin' men, Tom. What could we do against hired gunmen?" He shook his head gloomily. "Nobody here wants a shootin' fight. We all got families." He looked around the group, seeking their approbation and finding it, for their own logic was in his words.

"Any of you want to fight that bunch with guns?" Darby asked them.

Covertly they exchanged glances. One farmer grumbled unhappily, "Guns? My Gawd! It's already past time for plowin' for corn."

"You want to put your crop in for Drummond?" Houghton demanded.

"It probably ain't that bad."

"If it ain't, what are you doin' here?"

It was a dilemma they did not want to face, and again they sought refuge in an uneasy silence. Presently Houghton shifted in his chair and turned to Embree. "What's your idea on this, Embree?"

Instantly, they were watching Embree, on guard against him; they feared what he would say.

"I'd hate to push any man into a shooting fight," he said quietly.

"Still and all, we'd like your opinion."

He knew with the logic of long experience in such things that once Drummond had his hands on War Bow Valley, Spanish Spur would be cut back to the hill graze, and that when that happened, these farmers would have to go, for no organized force would exist to help them.

He began talking, softly, matter-of-factly, explaining all this to them; and they gave him their full attention, disliking his words, yet grudgingly believing. For some minutes he spoke, then concluded with quiet emphasis, "Unless Drummond's beaten, you'll all go, law or no law. Likely Spanish Spur and the smaller ranchers, too—we're all in the same boat."

"Amen," Jennings said soberly.

That worried stillness settled again on the room, to be broken at length by Darby. "Suppose we agree that's so. What do we *do*?"

"You can fight," Embree said. "You don't necessarily need guns to do it."

He saw the hope spring up in their faces and amplified his statement. "The auction on War Bow Valley comes off soon, and Spanish Spur will make a bid, but right now we can't match dollars with Drummond. If you people could raise a fund to help us, I believe we could beat him out." He paused, watching them intently, and added, "Of course, I'd give you promissory notes for your cash, and you'd have my word that you'd never have to worry about trouble with cattlemen again."

After he had spoken, it was some moments before a farmer raised his objection, saying, "But we've already paid for our patents. Why should we help a rancher buy the rest of it?"

"I've told you why," Embree replied patiently. "It's this or run from Drummond's guns in the end."

It was an unpleasant choice, and they could not decide. Presently a man at the table's end said, "We have faith in your word, Mr. Embree, but now we understand that Spanish Spur's split. Whom do you speak for?"

"For both partners."

Still they seemed unconvinced, and Darby voiced their last doubt. "We're all poor men, Embree, and while we might raise a little cash to help bid in the valley, we'd be running a big risk. Suppose, f'r instance, you leave, and some fire-eatin' gent takes ahold of Spanish Spur. Then what?"

"The Suttons would back any promise I made for them," Embree said earnestly.

Back in the shadows, a lanky farmer shifted his weight and rose slowly to his feet. "I'm agin' it," he stated flatly. "I was chased off a piece of land down in New Mexico because a rancher wanted my water. I've seen it happen in a dozen places, and I reckon some of you have, too. To hell with this idea! The cowman ain't been born that a farmer can trust."

Houghton swung around, protesting, but a murmur of agreement had swelled up and the tide had shifted, and with that Embree pushed off the wall, moving through the talk to the table where he stood, something in his still, cutting gaze silencing them.

"Talk's cheap," he said, in a low voice, "but look at you! Hiding behind barred doors and darkened windows to talk about what's rightfully yours! You shiver every time you see a man on horseback, and you run away from a fight like whipped dogs with your tail between your legs. Lord God! Don't you want to walk in the open, like men?" He paused, his eyes going from man to man. "You'll get no place against Drummond alone. For the last time: throw in with us, with guns or a bid on the Valley."

Their sour resentment of this judgment was plain on their faces, but Houghton cut in with quiet candor, "That's tough to swallow, but I'm afraid it's the straight medicine. Now, I move we call another meeting soon, with everybody in the Valley present. Meantime, we can talk this over with our neighbors and see if they'll help. How does it strike you fellows?"

After a moment there was a small grudging murmur of assent, and then others agreed, and with that they prepared to leave and the meeting was over. Embree turned toward the door, and Houghton called to him, "I'll get in touch with you, Embree," and Embree nodded and went on outside. The glum knowledge that nothing had been accomplished sat in him. All the way to Spanish Spur he was nagged by a feeling of having to fight with less than enough, but he never let it quite become an admission.

It was late when he arrived at the ranch, and as he threw off by the corral, Chuck came from the bunkhouse and stood near him in the darkness. Presently Chuck said laconically, "We're short a couple more hands."

"How's that?"

"Tal Evans and Wiley pulled out this evening after supper. Didn't even ask for their time. Said they didn't hanker to end up like Cal Sutton did."

"That's fine," Embree said ironically, "just fine." Then, after a pause, he added more soberly, "Still, maybe it's better that their kind goes."

"I just thought I'd tell you," Chuck said lamely.

"Sure, Chuck. Good night." Embree tramped off to the office, recalling with a secret bitterness how sincere was Amy's faith in him, and wondering how he was to justify it in the coming days.

Before dawn next morning Embree was in the saddle, his bags holding rations for a couple of days' roving. A half mile from the ranch he cut up into the Medicines, setting a northward course which brought him toward midmorning to a point over-looking Spanish Spur's high hill pasture. Many small meadows dotted the hills here, but as he rode on, studying them, he knew that they would never carry Spanish Spur's whole herd, should Drummond force them back to the hills.

The sun came above, its warmth brewing up the smell of pitch in the still thin air and running in small tangy waves through the silent glades of pines. Embree took out his pipe and smoked as he rode. After a while the hills turned into the northeast, and he kept on along their ridges, riding almost aimlessly but pausing frequently to watch the country, to study its activity, its changes. Miles north, and in the afternoon, he saw riders bunching cattle on a pasture of Box A, Sam Arnim's outfit; he waited until they hazed the herd southward toward Spanish Spur, and then he rode on, grim-faced. Once he cut over a high saddleback and sat for a space, studying the long narrow greenness of Lobo Valley, and toward four o'clock he passed high above Moorehead's ranch and noted its proximity to Arnim's range. Afterward he pushed on, studying in silence the trails he crossed, the movements of men and animals.

He camped that night somewhere in the hills above Box A's northern boundary, and the next morning's light found him still on high ground and swinging eastward. Toward ten o'clock he reached the juncture of the Medicines with the Bowstrings, being now above the northwest section of Spanish Spur range once more. Here, where two faint roads converged, leading northward into the Long Reach, he halted and observed the disreputable half town which bore the same name.

It was a shabby cluster of buildings on a narrow valley floor that stretched from the range country off into an indeterminate wilderness which was crisscrossed by a hundred hidden trails. There were a few ramshackle houses, a saloon and a rooming house, a store, and a gone-to-ruins blacksmith shop.

Embree got down, lit his pipe, and smoked reflectively for
some time as he contemplated the place. Presently he saw a pair
of riders coming along the road from the south, and after a while
he recognized Penn Drummond and his gunman, Bob Hackett.
These two rode into the town, got down, and entered the saloon,
Half an hour later they came out with others; Embree counted
eight. One of these men crossed to a house beyond the street, and
some minutes later came back with three more. The whole group
then held a brief parley, after which they mounted and rode out
of town, heading southward.

Embree had watched all this with close attention, and now he
again rose to the saddle and continued on his way, knowing that
Drummond was adding guns to his force. Two hours later, he
came to the Crippled Horse Branches, which watered this section
of Spanish Spur range. Here for some time he sat the saddle, staring pensively into the southwest, over the fifteen miles toward
the next nearest water—that finger of Buffalo Creek which tra-
versed War Bow Valley and without which only the Crippled
Horse Branches would be left to water all the stock over this vast
area: an impossibility. Having satisfied himself on that score, he
turned back the way he had come.

That night, Embree ate his cold meat and hardtack beside a
small fire again on the Medicines' east-west traverse; and in the
morning, knowing that he was near John Deane's homestead, he
dropped down out of the hills and rode to Deane's place.

Deane, who had eaten earlier, cordially offered him breakfast, and while Embree ate sat watching him and pulling on a
corn-cob pipe. Only when Embree had finished did Deane ask,
"You hear what happened down here day 'fore yesterday?"

"No, I've been in the hills."

"Drummond's riders busted up Darby's place," Deane said.
"Tore down his granary and ran their horses over his wheat, then
told him to get out of the country. From what I hear, his little girl
was hurt by one of their horses, too." He watched Embree.

Embree sat very still as he heard this news. Then he asked, "How do you know it was Drummond?"

"Tom Houghton saw 'em, too. They got into his wheat and Carl Hawley's after leavin' Darby's. Tom claims that fellow Hackett was headin' 'em, although they appeared to be a new crew."

Embree was remembering the bunch that Drummond had hired at Long Reach; he was thinking, too, of the meeting with the nesters and of their wishful belief that Drummond would leave them alone. "It was bound to come," he said slowly. He reached for his hat, rose, and added, "I'm sorry about Darby's girl. And—thanks, John. Thanks a lot." He started for the door.

"I guess you knew about the Sinks?" Deane asked.

Abruptly, Embree halted. "What about the Sinks?"

"Why, Drummond pushed a herd of cattle way in on your graze down there." Deane's eyes were watchful. "Didn't you know?"

"No," said Embree softly, "I didn't know." All at once caught by a sudden urgency, he went out, swung aboard, and broke his horse into a run out of the yard. He rode southward at a fast pace, crossing the Valley and splashing across Buffalo Creek where it came onto Spanish Spur range, and then, following the line between Spanish Spur and D Slash, he pushed due south for half an hour.

At last he sighted the D Slash herd that had invaded Spanish Spur range. They were grazing a mile on this side of the series of marshy pools at the low hills' edge, which, collectively, were known as the Sinks. Embree, swinging wide beyond them, pulled up and rested with his hand on the horn, adding it up. This was a test, a challenge, to let Drummond know how Spanish Spur would react following Cal Sutton's death. Failure to meet it would find D Slash stock moving steadily farther in, until they could not be pushed off and Spanish Spur choked to death under the sheer weight of Drummond's force.

A cold measured rage stirred up in Embree as he sat there; a tightness came about his mouth, and his eyes under his hatbrim were narrowed and stormy-dark while he weighed the implications of Drummond's latest move. Then, almost savagely, he jerked his horse's head around and drove in the spurs, heading for town where, he knew, he would find Penn Drummond.

As Embree sat the saddle surveying the scene at the Sinks, Sam Arnim, standing in the hallway of Amy's house in town, was having his own unsatisfactory moments. For the past twenty minutes he had been trying to elicit from Amy some clue as to her feelings for Jim Embree, and he had not succeeded. Being a jealous man, he was frustrated and angry, for he attributed his failure to sheer feminine guile on Amy's part: he firmly believed that it was a quality which all women possessed and used simply because they were women.

Now he regarded Amy with some dissatisfaction, repeating doggedly, "Regardless of what Embree thinks, Drummond's grown too big for you to buck, Amy. Your safest bet would be to sell out to me—and you know why."

She weighed that, not immediately rejecting it, then said, "But I believe in Embree. I think he can save Spanish Spur."

He searched her face, before he said more temperately, "Amy, I'd always hoped to marry you some day, and I know you wanted the same thing. But now it seems I've been a fool for thinking it."

"Sam, please—" Amy began.

"It's him—Embree—isn't it?"

"Don't be ridiculous!" Amy had grown weary of this shifting interrogation. "I feel about you just as I always have, Sam, but darn it, sometimes you'd try the patience of a saint!"

He colored a little, angered, but Amy's blue eyes were snapping with a temper of their own, and for some reason it mollified him to see that. Suddenly he smiled his surprisingly pleasing smile, which always seemed to make him another man.

He chuckled. "You're prettier when you're mad—if that's possible."

In spite of herself, Amy smiled, but she made a clucking sound with her tongue and said, "You are a case, Sam Arnim! Fairly jumping down my throat one moment and flattering me like a city drummer the next." Then she laughed with real amusement. "Now, get out of here! I've got school work to do."

Arnim allowed himself to be pushed to the door, but his dark mood lingered. As he stepped out on the porch he turned to regard her, then blurted with almost defiant candor, "To tell you the whole truth, it gives me fits to think that, after school's out, he'll be up at Spanish Spur, near you all the time, and me miles away." He blushed a little and added sheepishly, "Maybe that sounds like a kid, but it's the way I feel about you, and I can't help it."

Amy's eyes softened, and she said gently, "Yes, Sam, it sounds just like one of my fifth graders." But at his unhappy look she touched his arm and added, "Please don't act this way. Embree's my foreman—my chance to hold on. If you don't like him, at least try to understand."

He looked at her, then grinned abashedly. "I'll try. It's just that I'm a fool where you're concerned, and I guess I always will be. It was the way they made me, and I can't change it."

"No, it isn't," Amy said softly. "They made a pretty nice man in Sam Arnim—if he'd just let himself be."

He frowned, not understanding, but Amy said quickly, "Good-by, Sam," and closed the door, and after a moment he shrugged his big shoulders and trudged up the street, still puzzling over Amy's enigmatic words.

At the saloon he turned in, still full of his own dark juices, telling himself that he'd said what he had only to please Amy, and that was all. The whole thing could be ended so simply if only she would sell her share of Spanish Spur to him and marry him. He didn't want it for nothing—the money would always be hers, and it would be something saved from the wreck that Drummond was sure to bring about.

He saw Penn Drummond having a drink alone at the bar, and then he spied Taos and others of Drummond's crew at a poker table in back. Drummond nodded to him, motioning him back, and as he came up he offered, "I'll buy you a drink."

"And I'll take it," Arnim agreed dourly.

As he sipped his whisky, he felt Drummond's eyes on him, narrowly watchful. Presently the big man asked, "Why the long face?"

Arnim merely shrugged.

Drummond shifted around a little, saying softly, "Sam, it occurs to me that you're in a funny position in this country right now. Mind telling me exactly what it is?"

Slowly Arnim set his whiskey down and faced Drummond. "Just how do you mean?"

"Well," said Drummond, watching him steadily, "you're not with the farmers apparently, and it seems you're not on Embree's side."

"I'm not against him, either. I hate his guts, but I'm not against him."

"Now that's a hell of a position to take!" Drummond said disgustedly. "Just where do you stand?"

Arnim turned back to the bar, drank the rest of his whiskey, and said shortly, "I stand by myself. I'm taking no sides."

"And how long do you think that can last?"

Arnim was still for a moment, and then he turned, looking straight at Drummond. "You're a big man, Penn," he said evenly. "You might be big enough even to pull me to your side sometime. But not now. And I'd advise you not to try it just for the hell of it."

He saw the quick arrogant brightening come into Drummond's dark eyes, saw a harsh retort frame up; but it was suddenly cut short as Drummond's face changed and his glance went past Arnim's shoulder to the door.

Arnim waited a pair of seconds, then turned that way just as Embree pushed open the swinging doors and entered the saloon.

Embree paused momentarily inside, his eyes passing over the D Slash men in back and centering upon Drummond. Then he walked deliberately back that way and halted three paces from Drummond and Arnim He glanced briefly at Arnim, then turned to the other, saying abruptly, "Your cows are down on Spanish Spur beyond the Sinks, Penn. Get 'em off of there."

Suddenly, the game in back stopped. In the stillness, Drummond's face lighted with a slow wicked amusement. "Why, now," he drawled, "I didn't know that. Must have been a drift."

"That's a lie," Embree said softly. "You pushed 'em over there." Then, his eyes honing down to a dark sharp edge, "If you're not off that grass tomorrow, I'll drive you off. Moreover, I'm wiring the Sinks, and if any of your stock crosses the line, I'll shoot 'em."

It lay there, hard and implacable, for a brief space; then, before Drummond could answer, Embree wheeled and went toward the door. It had been quick, surprisingly final.

The tight shocked silence ran on for a moment after Embree had gone; then all at once Drummond turned toward his men, making a swift imperative inclination of the head, and Taos got up and cat-footed toward the rear room. All of this Sam Arnim saw and understood, and as Taos disappeared in back, he pushed his glass away over the bar and started for the front door.

"Stay back here, Sam," Drummond snapped.

Arnim kept on, saying curtly over his shoulder, "Go to hell. You don't run me, either."

Embree reached the boardwalk, ducked under the tie-up, and started across the street toward his horse, his anger only now leaving him; he was in the middle of the street when behind him he heard a soft urgent call. "Embree!"

He stopped and faced around, completely off guard, and then a wild alert shot through him, too late. At the corner of the alley below the saloon, full in the afternoon's sunlight, stood

Taos, his gun aimed at Embree, his face pale and pinched with a hate almost disfiguring in its intensity.

In the split second before Taos stepped forward, Embree heard the small metallic click as the gunman thumbed back the hammer; then, as Embree was about to take the long chance of going for his gun, another voice cut through the silence. "You're a dead man if you shoot, Taos! Put that gun away."

Out of the corner of his eye Embree saw Sam Arnim moving unhurriedly along the boardwalk, his gun trained steadily on Taos. The gunman dared not take his eyes off Embree, nor could he take the chance of firing with Arnim's threat hanging over him. For a moment he wavered; then, out of the dead silence, he snarled despairingly, "It's a trick!"

"Try it and see," Arnim urged quietly. "Better put up your gun."

He had moved out into the margin of the gunman's vision, and Taos slowly lowered his gun and eased the hammer down. There was malevolence in Taos' eyes such as Embree had seldom seen as the gunman looked at him across the dust; then, with his gun in the leather, Taos turned and stared stonily at Arnim, who stood his ground, waiting. Afterward, Taos again glanced toward Embree, saying thickly, "No matter. Another time." Then he went back up the alley.

Arnim holstered his gun, and after a moment Embree cruised on over the dust in his direction, stopping near the hitch rack. For some moments they studied one another, neither relenting, neither changing, and then Embree said, "Thanks, Sam."

He saw the withdrawn look come into Sam's gray eyes. After a moment, Arnim said, "I wouldn't want you to think you owe me a damn thing. I just don't like gunhawks."

"Whatever you say," Embree murmured, still watching him.

Arnim seemed to be considering this thing, trying to find a satisfactory explanation for what he had done. His face hard and deadly sober, he said, "What I mean is: I didn't do it for you. Suppose we leave it like that."

Without waiting for Embree's reply he turned and tramped up the way, his back ramrod-stiff.

Embree turned then and went back to his horse, mounted, and rode out of town. He had just been ready to revise a pretty well settled opinion of Sam Arnim when the man had shown his implacable dislike which was deeper than his act itself, and Embree had been left with his opinion unchanged. For just a moment he had the idea that Sam's explanation needed closer examination; then, with a sense of relief, he pushed that thought away: Arnim was making it easier all the time to dislike him.

He was halfway to Spanish Spur when it occurred to him that he'd never really wanted to dislike Sam until the open mention of Amy had come between them. Then it seemed to him what had been a simple world was turning into one with a thousand shades and colors, with a hundred unanswered questions that echoed like voices speaking down arched empty corridors.

CHAPTER SEVEN

B Y MIDAFTERNOON of the following day, Embree and his crew of four had strung wire for a quarter of a mile on either side of the Sinks, having hazed Drummond's cattle across the line in the morning. Since their arrival, Embree had been watchful for some move by Drummond and his men, but they had found no riders with the herd nor had any appeared as the day wore on, and gradually his vigilance relaxed. The fence was being erected on Spanish Spur land, and, while his challenge yesterday had doubtlessly angered Drummond, still he doubted that it would prompt the man to any overt action.

By noon, therefore, with the weight of the fencing job only half lifted from them, the men had decided to leave their guns and all necessary equipment at the tool wagon, and Embree did not object. With dinner over, he unbuckled his own gun belt and hung it over the horn of his saddle, and the crew then worked southward from the tool wagon, pushing the task in order to finish before evening.

They were intent upon their work a considerable distance from the wagon when, toward three o'clock, Chuck straightened abruptly, jerked his head toward the hills beyond the Sinks and said tersely, "Our company's comin'."

They turned and watched silently as the half dozen horsemen rode down into the flatland and came across the grass toward them at an unhurried lope. At their head rode Drummond, and Embree recognized Hackett and Taos among the others. As they came closer, he heard Chuck say softly, "And they catch us naked as jay birds, the artillery in the wagon."

"We're on our own land," he replied. "They won't start anything here."

It was a reassurance he did not himself feel; and when, at a few paces' distance, he read the hard businesslike cruelty on Drummond's rocky countenance, he knew with a sinking feeling that they had made a big mistake by leaving the guns behind.

Drummond and his bunch pulled up just beyond the wire, uttered no greeting, but surveyed the fence wordlessly, Drummond's face all the while growing darker as he stared at Embree.

"One thing I forgot to mention yesterday," Drummond said, with deceptive softness. "We're not used to fenced water in this country, Texas. It's not the custom."

"How about putting beef on another man's graze? That customary?"

"Ah," said Drummond. "I told you it was a drift, didn't I?"

Embree had no desire to pussyfoot through all that again. He said with a wintry finality, "You're not fooling with public land now, Drummond. Whatever right you have or claim don't go as far as Spanish Spur range. And I told you that yesterday, didn't I?"

"So you did," was Drummond's laconic reply. He looked away, both ways of the wire, said thinly, "I just wanted to see."

"And now you've seen. Anything else before you go?"

Only the hard glitter of Drummond's gaze betrayed his resentment; his face did not change as he said with slow malice, "Just a couple." And then, turning suddenly to his men, he almost shouted, "Cut that damn wire!"

Even as the words exploded, Embree made an involuntary lunge toward a shovel, but Hackett barked harshly, "Hold it!" Guns had come up in his hand and Taos', and he was grinning wolfishly at Embree, who had stopped and turned.

"Don't get rash," Hackett warned softly. "My little playmate here wouldn't mind a bit." He jerked his head at Taos.

A pair of Drummond's riders slipped from the saddle and walked toward the fence, one of them producing a pair of wire snippers. Behind Embree, Chuck was mumbling disgusted curses, and the faces of the Spanish Spur riders had gone still and waiting and a little frightened.

Drummond said, "Now just stand quiet, you fellows, and put your hands up." As they hesitated, he bellowed, "I mean it, by God!"

Slowly, they raised their hands, Embree last of all. A cold quiet fury was running wild in him, and a disgust even worse because he had walked into this with his eyes open. He said, "You're making the mistake of your life, Drummond. This fence is strung on Spanish Spur range."

"Yeah," Drummond growled, watching the wire cutting. "And I'm worried."

Quickly the two riders cut a gap in the wire, pulled the strands back, and then Drummond and his men rode through, Hackett and Taos the while keeping their guns steadily on Embree and his men. As they reached the other side they all dismounted, the riders lifting their ropes from their saddles. The two who had cut the wire now came back and Drummond turned, saying brusquely, "All right, tie these jokers' hands. I don't want any interference."

His men advanced on the Spanish Spur crew and began tying their hands behind their backs. They submitted, shame-faced. Chuck would have objected, but a Drummond man cuffed him hard in the mouth and growled. "Act your age and you won't get hurt."

A seething helpless rage filled Embree as he watched, and it was drowning the last of his judgment as they turned toward him and Taos said abruptly, "Bob, you cover 'em. I want to do this baby myself." So saying, the gunman holstered his gun, jerked a rope from another, and advanced on Embree, his face still and wicked; at the same moment, two others moved in back of Embree and waited.

Taos' face was in front of Embree with a hate on it almost indecent; a wave of revulsion hit Embree like a sudden sickness, and as the man closed in, he no longer cared what happened, and he brought his raised fists down in a smashing blow at Taos' face.

He heard Taos' startled cry, saw him go down, and then a driving weight slammed into his back. A pair of arms went around him, pinning his elbows at his side, he heard a low curse, and as he stiffened against that powerful hold from behind a rough voice rasped near his ear, "Better clip this chicken," and a hard weight crashed into his skull.

A roaring red agony tore through his head, his knees buckled, and he was gagging for breath, feeling himself supported only by those arms behind him. As from a distance Taos' snarling voice came at him. "Hold him up, hold him up, damn it!" And then the darting lights in his brain cleared and he was hauled upright and he saw Taos rise to one knee and then come scuttling toward him, a fist cocked.

The pain of that fist smashing into his lips blazed across his consciousness, clearing his head momentarily and he heard Drummond call sharply, "That's enough of that! I told you not to kill him, didn't I?"

Then his hands were being tied behind his back and his head came up, half-seeing, and Drummond was before him, a wicked gloating in his eyes, but once more Embree had to let his head drop from its sheer weight, from the pain in it.

"Embree! Can you hear me?"

He merely rolled his head on his neck, muttering through bruised lips, "Go to hell!" He heard Drummond's laugh.

"You're boot-tough, Embree," Drummond snarled. "But it's tough in the wrong direction, and I'm going to take some of it out of you!" He peered closely at Embree, then said brusquely to his men, "Take him over to that post and tie his hands to the top."

There was a kind of unreality about all this, because Embree could scarcely move his limbs as they dragged him to the post, yet he was aware of everything. His wrists were being lashed to the top of the post, and he felt a senseless lost rage and a violent disgust at his weakness: his bitterness was an almost determinate thing, having, it seemed, form and palpability.

"I hope you can hear me, Texas," Drummond was saying tauntingly. "If you get over this, get to hell out of the country—understand? If you don't, the next time it'll be a bullet."

Drummond was lashing himself into a rage, and Embree knew what was coming; he heard Drummond speaking again.

"And you others, watch close, because if you're in the country tomorrow, you'll get the same thing."

Embree's mind was saying dully, "Get it over with. Get started," and then the first hissing slash of the whip struck his back and he cried out with the pain. He summoned all his strength and clenched his teeth against the raw searing agony of what would follow, and with the next three blows he merely shook; after that a soft warm flood ran over his mind and down into his legs, and he knew no more as his weight fell against the thongs about his wrists.

He hung there, and the lash tore his shirt away, and the blood oozed out of the welts on his back, and still Drummond plied the whip, his lips in a tight snarl, his breath coming hard and labored. Then all at once Hackett stepped forward and grabbed his arm, saying queerly, "You told us yourself you didn't want him killed."

Drummond stopped short and looked at him vacantly. "That's so." His obsession left him, he let the whip fall to the ground, and he ran his sleeve over his forehead, wiping at the beading of sweat brought out by his exertion. Then he turned to the Spanish Spur riders.

"That's a sample," he said hoarsely. "Anybody who works for your outfit can expect the same thing. Now, get up there to your horses and ride! And when you go, head out of the country. Untie 'em, boys."

They stood there pale and bemused by the raw brutality of what they had witnessed, and as their bonds were loosened they moved away tight-lipped, going toward their horses. Drummond and his crew watched them go and waited until they had mounted and ridden away, in the opposite direction from Spanish Spur. Only then did Drummond's hard intensity relax, and he let go a long breath, saying with some satisfaction, "Well, that takes care of them," and walked to his horse.

When they had mounted and were ready to leave, it was Hackett who, with a glance at Embree's still form slumped against the post, asked, "Ain't you goin' to untie him, Penn?"

"Let him hang!" Drummond said with scalding hate. "If the buzzards or coyotes don't get him, he'll crawl out of this country now. I don't care which it is."

Embree was first aware of the papery dryness of his mouth and of a dull ache that began at the base of his skull and went through his whole head; then, as sensitivity grew in him, that misery merged with a stiff burning pain that lay over his whole back, and he realized that he was lying on his stomach, stretched out upon some soft surface with his head turned sidewise. A corner of his mind registered these impressions, and he lay awhile letting them grow stronger and then opened his eyes.

Amy sat a few feet from him, slowly rocking and staring into the fireplace, and he saw that he was in the living room of the ranch house, lying on the sofa, but was puzzled by his manner of coming here. He lay very still, wondering about it, while his attention remained fixed upon Army.

She was dressed in a red wrapper pulled tightly around her nightgown, and her arms were folded over her breasts, which softly rose and fell to her breathing. He watched the light from lamp and fire shine on her hair and face while her eyes rested on the flames.

He had this long look and then started to rise, and the involuntary groan which it cost him jerked Amy's attention to him at once. She got up, came near the sofa, and stood looking down at him with concern.

"Don't try to get up," she said firmly. "In fact, the doctor says that you're to sleep right there tonight." Then she paused. "How do you feel?"

"I've felt better," he said thickly.

She nodded slowly, her eyes darkening. "Now you mind me," she said, left the room, and presently came back and knelt by him, holding a glass of water and two white pills.

"You're to take these. I'll hold the glass low, and you open your mouth." She gave him the pills and stood over him, supporting the glass while he drank, and afterward he closed his eyes. When he reopened them Amy was sitting on a small stool near the sofa, watching him, her face shadowed and soft.

"How did I get here?" he asked.

"Chuck brought you. The other hands rode out of the country, I guess, but he came back after they'd left and brought you here. Then he came to town for me and the doctor."

Embree's eyes were clouding with the memory of what had happened, and small refined points of anger were coming into them. She saw him drawing together and hardening his spirit, and she said, very low, "Embree, I—I'm so awfully *sorry*! If I hadn't asked you to stay..." Her voice trailed off, the sound of regret lingering.

There was a darkness, a tenderness in her eyes that again made him sharply aware of her; it was like suddenly discovering the fine qualities of a thing long known but only newly appreciated. But he said with a kind of gruffness, "I wanted to stay, too, so don't blame yourself." He paused, looking away. "It actually doesn't hurt too bad, and in a way I'm sorry. I don't want to forget it for a long, long time."

For an interval then she remained silent and indrawn, because it had struck her powerfully that this man's stubborn unbeaten ways could easily cause his death; she was wondering how far she would influence him in what he might do, and what the results of his actions might be.

When she spoke, it was with a slow sadness. "I don't always understand men's reasons for doing things, for they are the reasons of men and I am a woman. I'm a little worried now, because I think you will fight Drummond for revenge, and that's a poor reason for doing anything."

"There are other reasons," he told her.

"Of course there are." She turned her head a little, seeming to think of that. Her face was in the light now, and he saw that her eyes had a dark coloring, almost a deep violet. Without turning her face she murmured, "But which reason is the most important to you? That's a thing you ought to decide. Why should Spanish Spur mean enough to you to risk your life for it?"

A few short days ago, he might have told her that a rider's ranch is his home and that he will fight to defend it as such; but now, this was not the whole answer. He was learning the rest of it from her, from the way she looked at him on occasion, and from the things he had only begun to see in her since Cal Sutton's death. She had the power to sharpen the moments when he was near her, to make all the appetites grow keen, to make old forgotten thoughts seem like new; yet he knew that he had begun to search for this in her, and that he might be finding it where it did not exist for him. Loneliness would do that to any man, and he had been lonely a long time.

She turned to look at him. "Why should it, Embree?" she repeated.

Be careful, he told himself. And then Amy saw the taciturnity come over him, changing his face and veiling those piercing eyes. "Everyone likes to feel that he's needed, I guess," he told her, weighing his words. "You told me that I was needed here, and there's no place else in the world that that's true."

After a while he heard her sigh, and then she rose and went to the table and turned down the wick, throwing shadows over the room; she swung to face him and looked at him a long moment before she said softly, "That was a nice way of saying it. Good night, Embree." And she left.

Embree lay staring into the fire, disturbed by the sense of change in and around him. It came to him that even though this were so, it could lead nowhere: he was in danger of making a fool of himself. Then he shut his mind tight on that conclusion and fell asleep.

Amy returned to town the next day, and for four days thereafter Embree lazed about the ranch, giving his back a little time to heal. But on the fifth morning he saddled and left Spanish Spur, cutting up into the hills and, once across their crests, riding down into Lobo Valley.

He arrived at Stacey Jennings' place, his immediate destination, around ten o'clock. Jennings came out on the porch as Embree rode into the yard and asked him down for coffee, which Embree declined with thanks. Leaning against a support post, Jennings eyed Embree with a steady interest and said with good-natured wonder, "I didn't expect to see you around for a while, fellow."

"I'm like a buckskin mule." Embree grinned with a flash of white teeth. "Hard to hurt and fast to mend." Then, leaning forward on the horn, "Stacey, you bought chips that day that Meeker was killed, and later you stayed a round for that nester meeting at Houghton's. How does your hand look now?"

Jennings dropped his cigarette butt and ground it out beneath his boot, then raised his slow glance. "Well, I'll tell you," he said carefully. "I'm no man to run from a fight, nor to fear admitting it when I'm licked." He hesitated, then added with complete candor, "Right now I'm trying to figure out if Drummond's won this thing or not."

"He hasn't got War Bow Valley. The rest of it won't mean a thing in the long run."

"Ah," said Jennings softly, "but why wouldn't he get it? Don't misunderstand me, now. But you'll need money, and McVickers in at the bank has to get Drummond's permission to buy an extra cigar. As for the nesters"—his lip curled in mild scorn—"don't count on any money from them."

"Why not?"

Jennings shrugged. "They've been catching hell proper. The day you had your trouble, Drummond's wild bunch rared down through there, cutting fences and trampling crops and generally raising Ned." He shook his head. "I'm sorry for those folks; they're not bad people. But they're scared, and I don't blame 'em."

After a moment Embree asked softly, "Sure some of it hasn't rubbed off on you, Stacey?"

"Don't let your mad at Drummond spoil your judgment," Jennings said, with a touch of stiffness. "I'm no Frank Moorehead."

"What about Moorehead?"

"Why, he sold out."

"To Drummond?"

"No, to Sam Arnim."

For some moments Embree sat very still on the leather, his dark eyes on the smother of morning haze which was rising under the sun's heat down the valley. He was thinking that Moorehead had a perfect right to sell and Arnim to buy, but in a sense Arnim was contributing to the feeling of Drummond's invincibility that was running through this country—both by buying out Moorehead and in his insistence that Amy sell out to him. He had this unsatisfactory reverie, his resentment of Arnim growing deeper the while, and then he looked up and saw Jennings watching him narrowly, and he said, "Frank was a wishy-washy fool, anyhow. Well, thanks for the pow-wow." He reined about and started on.

"Hold on a minute," Jennings called, and as Embree stopped his horse and faced about Jennings said, "Just want to remind you—in case you need some help, you know where to come."

Embree said, "Thanks, Stacey. I won't forget that, or the fact that you made the offer." He rode on.

He had never doubted that these present troubles had been merely preliminary skirmishes, for always at the bottom of everything else lay the hard fact that whoever controlled War Bow Valley controlled the country. Drummond's present campaign had two purposes : to keep Spanish Spur off balance, and to drive the farmers from the Valley. By doing the second of these things, Drummond would prevent a combination from forming against him and also be free to grab up the land the farmers might abandon. And now, with the news of Moorehead's having sold out, it appeared that the pressure was going beyond the farmers, reaching even to the small ranchers.

These things Embree considered carefully as he left Lobo Valley, crossed the east-west traverse of the Medicines, and dropped down into the small trading center of Stoneman's Store, the heart of the Valley farming region. As his horse splashed up a spray crossing the creek behind Stoneman's, he saw a farmer step around the store's corner, take a look, and then duck back out of sight. He smiled grimly at that; and as he rounded the building he saw a dozen farmers lined up on the long porch, their weather-beaten faces both taciturn and grimly watchful.

Waving a short greeting to them, Embree rode to the rack, taking their short nods as his welcome. He got down and hitched unhurriedly, then tramped over to the porch and came up among them. He looked them over slowly as he took his pipe from his pocket and lit it, before saying casually, "I'm here to hire hands. Anybody want a job?"

In the silence after his words a man said spitefully, "I wouldn't wonder you need men. Saw three of your fellows ridin' out the other day, and they looked kinda pale and shaky. What they told us wasn't much of a recommendation for workin' at Spanish Spur."

Embree nodded, letting the smoke curl up past his eyes. "Just so. They're not the kind of men I want."

"Drummond didn't either, did he?" a farmer asked, pointedly sly.

Embree swung his head around and then his body. He stared at him and said flatly, "To hell with Drummond. You fellows ever going to get him out of your craw?"

He could feel it then : the shame and anger, the dogged miserable dissatisfaction that was eating at these men like a disease. The silence drew on, and then a young fellow in the doorway moved up a little and spoke. "I think I'll take the job."

He was a tall young man with sandy hair and work-corded arms, and now he said to Embree by way of explanation, "Name's Will Howell. Drummond's crowd spoiled our wheat, and I'd a sight rather work for somebody who fights that dirty son than stay here and let him push me around." His glance went around the group, conveying his full meaning.

As though they had been waiting for just this, a pair of men at the end of the porch came forward, one of them saying, "We're in the same boat. I'm Fred Kraft, and this is Vance Ketchum. We'll take the job if you want us, although we're not cow hands."

"No matter. I want you, all three," said Embree. Then, to the others, "If you know anybody else who wants to hire on, send 'em to me." He added, not without sarcasm, "I won't tell Drummond who sent 'em."

A man among the farmers retorted dryly, "Mighty funny! But tell the joke to Drummond—here he comes."

Embree saw the men stiffen and turned to see Drummond and a pair of riders coming at a lope down the road from up-valley.

A complete silence settled on the porch as they slowed up, came on to the store at a walk, and halted their horses. Although there were a dozen men here, Drummond's hot angry attention sought out Embree and held, while Embree returned his stare steadily through lids that had narrowed a little.

With a musing kind of vexation, Drummond said, "Damn it, do I have to do it all over again?"

"You won't try," Embree said, quietly contemptuous. "You're only three to one."

Almost impersonally, Drummond seemed to study him, reserving some harsh judgment as he let the words pass. Then he shifted on the leather and spoke peremptorily to Sim Darby. "You, Darby. Tell Harve Morgan I was by his place with the money. If he's still of a mind to sell, he can come to town now; I'm running no errands for him." He hesitated, his glance running over them and humbling them with its contempt. "That goes for the rest of you, too. When you're ready to sell, you can come to me."

Out of the shamed silence that followed, Will Howell said with dry wrath, "On our knees, or kin we walk?"

As Drummond swung around, frowning, Embree said, "Be quiet, Howell. Let this damned turkey strut and puff, because he won't do any worse unless he's got his gunmen at his back."

One of Drummond's riders muttered an oath and squared around on the saddle, but Drummond snapped, "Shut up!" He realized that he was just on the point of becoming ridiculous, here, and grew cautious; yet his eyes were still and mean as he looked at Embree.

"You should have taken my advice, Texas. Any way you play it, you'll follow those hands of yours out of the country before long."

"No," Embree said quietly, "I've got some men who don't scare now. I'll be around long enough to take my licking out of your hide."

But a new grim interest flashed across Drummond's face. "Who'd you get?"

Without prompting, the three men whom Embree had hired moved forward a little, staring straight and hard at Drummond. He looked them over for a long moment, then said in a wintry tone, "Boys, you were warned—you're not going to like that job. You're not going to like it a little bit!" And suddenly he jerked his horse around, broke it into a run, and rolled up the valley, followed by his men.

Embree watched them go, growing smaller behind the golden tendrils of dust weaving slowly across their wake, and presently he turned and looked at the three men who had just cast their lot with Spanish Spur. "He means that," he told them quietly. "There'll be more trouble. I won't hold you to your word."

Will Howell made a gesture. "We've already had some trouble," he said. "A little more can't hurt. Let's go."

They moved down the steps, going after their horses at the side of the store, while the farmers on the porch watched them with a glum kind of indecision. As Embree stepped to the saddle he was almost smiling, and then the men rode around to join him and he turned a little and bent a sardonic look on those standing on the porch.

'Don't feel too bad, boys," he jeered softly. "Maybe Drummond will let you ride to town for the money, when he buys you out."

As he wheeled his horse and rode away, he took with him the sharp memory of their bleak hopeless faces, faces in which, however, some powerful anger was beginning to leaven the despair. He hadn't really wanted to taunt them, but perhaps it had helped, after all. He would see.

CHAPTER EIGHT

Tom Houghton was alone, reading a two-weeks-old news-paper by the light of a lantern on his table, when it came. It hit as a pounding rush of hard-spurred horses through the night, and a sudden racket of savage yells, punctuated by the crackling of gunfire. In the first moment a bullet shattered the window pane and plowed on into the opposite wall, and even as the crash came Houghton threw himself to the floor, knocking over the lantern and killing the light in a purely reflex action as he fell. He lit off balance, cursing under his breath, and a quick runnel of fear shot up his spine, to be drowned by the sudden outraged anger that rushed through him as he realized that this was Drummond's bunch.

For a moment he lay there, trembling, the steady pound-ing of the guns sending a hail of lead through the window and splatting into the doors and walls. Then, drawing a breath, he got to hands and knees and scuttled to the corner where he kept his carbine, feeling better the minute his hand touched the cool barrel. As he turned, levering in a shell, he caught the growing shimmering-red reflection on the night's darkness, beyond the window, and knew that his buildings had been fired. Gritting his teeth, he darted to the window and shoved the carbine's barrel over the sill.

Out there, the shifting figures of horsemen moved in and out against the mounting blaze of the corn crib and the wagon shed, and Houghton had to draw a long breath to steady himself against the wrath that was shaking him. Then he found a rider in his sights and pulled the trigger, and a sharp yell went up and the rider threw up his arms convulsively and toppled from the leather.

At that, a howl of rage went up in the yard, the gunfire rose up stronger, and a wild unrecognizable voice yelped indignantly, "Fire the damn house! He's alive in there, and he got Reb."

Bullets splintered the logs near the window, their breath sighing past Houghton's face. He spied a figure running across the yard with an oil can, he shot at it and missed, and the figure passed out of his view; then he heard the liquid slosh against the door.

Someone in the yard was shouting through the confusion, "Bring one of them burning two-by-fours! Pitch it on the roof!"

All at once, Houghton realized that he couldn't stay here, and he turned from the window just as a heavy weight struck on the roof overhead. Tiny flames already were licking under the door, and in a few minutes the shack would be an inferno. He fired one more shot, then wheeled and ran for the lean-to at the rear of the shack, a voice outside cutting sharp into his consciousness. "That'll do it—to hell with him! Let's move on to Spanish Spur."

Houghton pushed through the lean-to and out into the open air, running. Twenty yards back in the darkness he stopped and turned, his breath coming fast with excitement and with a sobbing kind of rage. A wrath as deep as the night and as black shook him, as he viewed his place burning. He knew that he could save nothing, even if they went immediately, which they would not. The figures of Drummond's raiders swirled through the smoky reflections like the imps at some infernal orgy, and suddenly Houghton felt the unashamed tears on his cheeks, tears of shock and rage: three years of his life, of his hardest labor, were going up in smoke and flame back there, and he thought with a desolate unbelieving wonder, Why! It'll all be done within a few minutes!

Then only did he become aware of a horse cropping grass near him in the darkness. He turned, looking at its dark shape, and then he felt his anger refined, channeled in a way that came almost as a relief from pain.

Slowly, he began moving in the direction of the horse, making soft soothing sounds; it threw up its head and watched him, then went back to munching grass. He touched its head and stroked it, caught the bridle, and patted its neck to gentle it. The animal, he now saw, was saddled—probably the horse ridden by the man he had shot.

After another moment he stepped into the saddle and lifted the reins, and the animal answered them brightly. For a few yards Houghton went at a walk, the racket back there hitting him almost like a physical pain, and then he booted the horse into a run.

They intended now to move on to Spanish Spur, believing him dead or afoot and cringing somewhere in the darkness: such was their uncaring arrogance. But while they would follow the level ground around the Medicines, he could take the direct course to Spanish Spur, crossing into Lobo Valley and then traversing the trail over the Medicines which led almost into Spanish Spur's yard. With luck, he would reach Embree before Drummond's night raiders got there; and then—he would have something more to say to them.

All at once he laid the leather against the horse's withers, simultaneously pounding his boots into its flanks, and the animal gave a quick grunt and settled down into flight.

Brad had come home completely and surprisingly sober and, after supper, had spent a couple of hours with Embree in his office, discussing ranch matters and going over the tally and record books with him. Embree had begun by being warily pleased, but a reluctant suspicion had begun to harden in him as it became apparent that Brad was interested chiefly in knowing about the number of marketable cattle on Spanish Spur range.

Embree sat now, watching Brad as he reread the tally books. He told Brad, "Of course, those figures are probably off a little, one way or the other, until we have spring roundup."

"And can't we?"

Embree raised an eyebrow. "With everything that's happened? Late rain and cold, your father killed, and now this ruction with Drummond?"

Brad nodded. "I guess that's so."

Embree laced his fingers behind his head, leaned back in his chair, and inquired softly, "You figurin' on sellin', Brad?"

Brad threw him a quick glance.

"If you are," Embree went on evenly, "I'll have to remind you that Cal wanted the ranch to hang together. Besides, Amy wants that, and I doubt that she'd agree to your selling."

Brad was watching him with a mild resentment. "I've talked to Amy. And although I don't intend to sell, I'd have a perfect right to if I wanted to."

"Well, well," Embree murmured. "Did you go to the trouble to find out?"

Brad colored a little. Then he said, "As a matter of fact, I did. What of it?"

Embree turned slowly in his chair, closed the tally books, and shoved them back on the desk, his mouth tightening. Then he pushed up to his feet and faced Brad.

"I guess it's about time we understood one another, Brad," he said, in a soft drawl. "Suppose we begin by your telling me when you're going to start doing something for Spanish Spur."

"No sermons, Embree," said Brad darkly.

"I'm not going to preach. I've never said anything to you about your ways because Cal didn't, and Amy just acts as though there's nothing wrong where you're concerned. I guess that's their business. But my business is to hold this outfit together, and I think there's plenty wrong."

"Like what?" Brad demanded resentfully.

Embree hesitated, for he knew only that Brad drank and gambled, and that he was seeing Lily Farnum with some regularity—for what that was worth. Now that he had to mention it critically, it all seemed innocent enough, save that it added up to a negative attitude toward Spanish Spur which, in itself, he found intolerable. Even as he admitted that to himself, Embree said, "You hang around in town all the time, gambling too much and drinking more than you should. Moreover, it's common knowledge that you see Lily Farnum——"

"Leave her out of this!" Brad said instantly, his face hardening.

Embree's gaze sharpened, and after a moment he said, "All right, nothing intended there." He took a step toward Brad. "But I'm telling you this, Brad: as long as Amy wants Spanish Spur to stay one ranch, I'll keep it like that. Up to a certain point, you can do as you please, but when you do anything to hurt your sister—like selling out and breaking up the outfit—you answer to me!"

Brad was staring at him with angry baffled wonder. After a brief interval he murmured, low and incredulous, "You—Amy? Well, I'll be damned!"

"Damned if you won't," Embree assured him.

A reply was ready on Brad's lips, and then it died as they both heard the ragged run of a horse coming into the yard—a tired broken rhythm of hoofs that shouted of urgency. Embree took time to say tersely, "Remember, Brad!" and then headed for the door, and in a moment Brad followed.

By the time Embree reached Houghton, Chuck and the other hands had come from the bunkhouse and surrounded the farmer, and as Embree joined them Chuck turned to him. "Embree, Houghton claims Drummond's bunch is headin' up this way for a raid——"

They all began to talk, until Embree called for quiet and said to Houghton, "What about this, Tom?"

Houghton slid from the saddle, and in short angry snatches he told his story. "I can't be too far ahead of them," he concluded. "I'd say there's not much time."

They were all silent, looking at Embree. The first thing he said was, "I'm sorry for you, Tom. There's a place for you here if you want to stay." Then, to the others, in an unhurried tone, "You boys light all the lamps in the bunkhouse and then bring your guns and come up on the porch. Tell the cook to come along, too, because the bunkhouse won't be healthy for a while. Now, hop to it."

He went to his office and strapped on his own gun, killed the light, and when he returned to the house the men were waiting on the steps. He told them almost casually, "This oughtn't to be too hard. Just pick cover behind the porch posts and don't try to be a hero. They'll slam into the bunkhouse, thinking we're there, and then we'll pepper 'em. They won't take much of it."

Off in the distance sounded the small growing thunder of running horses, and they went up the steps and scattered along the porch, taking their positions in the darkness.

The sound of the bunch of horsemen grew along the night, and finally Embree could see the dark moving mass of them bulking sharper against the lighter darkness. Then a man's high "Ai-e-e-e-e" split the night, and their rush brought them full into the yard. A gun shouted, and another, glass crashed and jingled, and Bob Hackett's form flashed through the light from a bunkhouse window—Hackett standing high in his stirrups as his harsh voice hammered, "Smoke 'em out! Smoke 'em out!"

As Hackett lifted his defiant shout, the lean hard crack of a rifle sounded down the porch from Embree, and he thumbed back his hammer and fired at the bunch of horsemen. Instantly the sound was followed by the full ragged blast of other guns firing almost in unison. At the first shot a rider jerked, grabbed wildly at the horn, bent over, then fell leadenly toward the ground as his horse shied away and pitched his body free of the saddle.

For a few moments there was a wheeling, cursing confusion in the yard. A voice, which Embree recognized as Hackett's, sang out angrily, "They're in the house! Get down and find cover!"

But the fire from the porch, deliberate and wicked, kept them off balance. A horse screamed, high and anguished, pitched, throwing its rider, who lit in a crumpled heap and dragged himself along the ground. The animal went bucking away into the darkness, scattering the others and adding to the confusion.

A few men were firing toward the house. A bullet struck the post near Embree, caromed away with a long whine, and somewhere down the porch's darkness he heard a quick groan and a voice said unsteadily, "Damn it! I'm hit——"

It had all happened in the span of a few seconds, and now, laced with bitter disgust, a man's voice rose from the melee. "Two men dropped in one night's enough—let's go!" There came the scuffling beat of horses spurred hard, the dark mass of riders boiled and shifted and broke, and some of them ran for it.

Hackett's angry shout followed them. "Come back here, you yellow bellies!" But under the searching fire of Spanish Spur the remaining group made a brief run across the yard, throwing back lead wildly and harmlessly as they went. In the area beyond the light they spread a little, exchanged a few desultory shots, and then, as abruptly as it had begun, the fight ended, and Embree heard the run of their horses going off into the night.

After a while he got up, slipped his gun into the holster, and went toward the steps. Dark figures came that way from up the porch, and he asked, "Who got hit?"

"Me," said Howell, in a pinched voice. "Creased my arm—but damn it all if it don't sting!"

They moved down the steps into the yard. Embree sent a pair of them to find out if Hackett had taken his wounded with him and told the others to go to the bunkhouse for coffee. In his office he found salve, a bottle of whisky, and cloths, and returned to the bunkhouse, where he cleaned and bandaged Howell's wound, which was superficial.

They sat down to coffee as the two hands returned to report no sign of the wounded. And at that moment, and for the second time that night, they heard the commotion of approaching horses. They raised startled faces, listening and almost unbelieving. Suddenly Chuck blurted, "My God! No end to this?" and pushed back his chair and the others, too, went for their guns.

Embree said tersely, "Don't go off half cocked, lots of people ride horses. Here go the lights!" and he blew out the lamp and signaled the cook to do likewise with the light in the cookshack. Afterward, he went in darkness toward the door where he waited, holding the door half open.

There was no drive, no spurring urgency behind this new cavalcade; the group of horsemen came at a trot, slowed to a walk, and pulled up in the yard's center. Embree could see that there were eight or ten of them, and then one of them said peevishly, "By God, it's as black as the inside of a cat! Nobody around? I could have sworn all that shootin' racket came from up this way."

"It's all right, Sim." Embree had recognized Darby's voice. "We just weren't sure who you were." So saying, he went out into the yard, and with that the farmers reined over his way a little and stopped, and once more the light in the bunkhouse came on. The hands began drifting outside.

In the faint light hitting them, Embree detected the grimness of their faces. These farmers were mad deep down inside them, and it gave him an odd satisfaction, a kind of justification, to see it.

"Shootin' up this way, wasn't there?" Darby asked.

"A little. Drummond's bunch raided us, but there was no harm done," Embree told him. "We were ready for him."

"We weren t!" Darby said, with considerable disgust. He spied Houghton. "Tom, your place is——"

"I know, I know," Houghton cut in wearily.

"Just thought I'd tell you," Darby said lamely. "But you're not the only one who caught it down the Valley tonight. That's why we're here." He shifted, facing Embree. "We've waited too long. You were right, Embree, and I for one wish we hadn't wasted time. Still, maybe it ain't too late."

"There's some time left," Embree said soberly. The recollection of their vacillations, their indecisiveness came back to him, although he could see none of that in them now.

"Then I'll get to the point," Darby was saying. "Drummond's gone clear beyond all bearing. We're takin' you up, Embree. We'll raise some money to help bid in the Valley, maybe twelve—fifteen thousand dollars, and we'll fight with you too if it comes to that." He swung around, facing the others. "Right?"

They muttered their agreement.

"In other words," Darby added, "We're in it with you, right through to the bitter end."

Embree waited a moment before he said soberly, "I'm glad you've finally seen it that way. I don't think you'll be sorry."

"Just one thing," Darby qualified. "We think we speak for everybody, but we want to make sure. We've called a meeting down at Stoneman's tomorrow after everybody's through work, and we'll make you definite pledges then—settle the whole shootin' match, once and for all."

"I'll be at Stoneman's," said Embree. And then he added, "Of course you've got to keep this quiet, be careful who you tell about it."

"We know that," said Darby gruffly. "Good night." He raised his hand in farewell, pulled on the reins, and the farmers wheeled about and rode out of the yard. Embree watched them go, wondering why he felt none of the satisfaction that he should have experienced. He started for the bunkhouse, but a thought rose from deep in his mind and he hauled up and looked around the group.

"Where's Brad?"

"Why," Houghton began, looking around, "he was here just a minute ago—standin' right by me. Must be in the bunkhouse."

But Brad was not in the bunkhouse. After ascertaining that, Embree bade his men good night and went on to the office, and afterward he went into the house itself, finding it dark and deserted. Then he came back to the porch and stood staring narrowly down into the darkness of the yard. The night wind off the hills eddied about him with a cool freshness, stirring up only a strange discontent in him. After a while he went down to the corral where Brad's horse had stood, saddled, since he had ridden out from town. The horse was gone.

Embree paused a while there in the darkness, carefully thinking back, and then he remembered that he had seen Brad standing out a little from the edge of the crowd, intent on Darby's words as the farmer promised aid in bidding on the Valley and spoke of the meeting at Stoneman's.

After that, Embree realized, he had seen no more of him.

Lily Farnum admitted Brad. As he kissed her she returned his embrace with a warmth that both surprised and gratified him; and afterward she went with him into the living room's light and stood observing him closely before she asked, "Isn't it rather late to be back in town, Brad?"

"Maybe so." He was looking at her queerly, and there was something in his eyes that caused her presently to think, Why, he's changed—something has happened to him!

"What is it, Brad?" she asked. "You seem—well, strange."

Brad, still watching her, said slowly, "Lily, I'm trying to make up my mind whether I'm a damned scoundrel or just a plain fool about a good-looking woman."

Something like fear flitted through her hazel eyes, and she asked in a small voice, "Meaning me? Would a man have to be a fool to like me?"

"You know what I mean!" A tortured impatience was in Brad's voice. All at once he took a step toward her. "Listen to me, Lily: out there tonight Drummond's bunch pulled a raid, and Jim Embree—a fellow who gets paid for it—fought 'em off. Off my ranch. That's not all, either. Drummond's been kicking those poor damned farmers around like so many dogs, and in a way I've been helping him." He paused, shook his head, then turned away, saying with bitter disgust, "I've had about enough of myself, Lily. I've reached the place where I can't stand it unless I'm drunk as a boiled owl half the time." He wheeled, staring at her in hard wonder. "What have you done to me, anyhow?" he murmured.

She stood very still and straight, thinking, And what would his opinion of me—and himself—be if he knew that I had sold his chance remark to Drummond, and possibly caused his father's death?

As she looked at this boy who loved her, and whose love she had not at first wanted, she felt a constriction around her heart that rose and seemed even to close her throat against words. And then, even while she dredged up the determination to go on with the game, she found herself saying, "It doesn't sound funny to me at all, Brad. I—I believe I would feel the same way."

He turned his incredulous look upon her, and under it she wavered. She had now only to tell him the truth, suffer his contempt, and watch the hurt and remorse have its way with him. And then, desperately, she was telling herself that he must never know, that somehow she would find a way out of this dilemma for both of them, some way to break Penn Drummond's blackmailing hold....

Quickly she came around the table, close to Brad, her eyes filling with reproach. "Haven't we talked this over before?" she asked, low, pleadingly. "You've told me yourself that Drummond will win this fight, that Spanish Spur will have to sell or grow smaller. What about us then? Where would you get the money to do what we've planned, Brad?"

He stood staring miserably at her, and then he shook his head. "The old man wanted Spanish Spur to keep going—Amy and I running it together. Embree told me that, plainly. How can I do something like this and not tell Amy?"

"And if you told her, Embree would put a stop to it the next minute!" She waited, her face changing a little, and then she sighed and turned away. "I—I suppose it was foolish of me to even think——"

Brad made a wounded sound and reached for her, drew her fiercely to him, and when he kissed her the tenderness of her response drove away his last doubts. At last he held her away, his eyes searching her face.

"Lily, Lily, is this *real*? You *will* go away with me?"

For a moment she could not meet his eyes; she was thinking bitterly, more real than you'll ever know, Brad. And then she told him, in a low unsteady voice, that which was no lie. "I swear that I will go."

A moment longer he looked at her, and then decision came into his face. "All right. I'll give Drummond the option, and I'll sell as soon as he gets the Valley."

He turned and strode across the room and back, underlining his words with a kind of anger.

"Tell him that. And tell him, too, that Embree is meeting the farmers at Stoneman's tomorrow night to get their help in raising money for a bid on War Bow Valley." He swung around, facing her, and added dryly, "And if Amy tried that with *half* of Spanish Spur, she would be sunk!" They looked straight at one another.

"Yes-yes, I'll tell him," Lily said.

There was a stillness, and she realized that it had been done; she walked to the door with Brad, scarcely hearing what he was saying, and then she was seeing the misery in his eyes as he said haltingly, "Maybe—when we're married—this will seem all right?"

It was her last chance. She did not take it, but murmured in a barely audible voice, "Yes—when we are married," and he went out.

She sent Juan for Drummond, and when, some time later, he arrived Lily was sitting at the table, her face tight and pale. He greeted her, but she merely looked up at him in a distant manner and said, "You will find Brad Sutton at the hotel. He's ready to give you the option."

A broad grin spread across Drummond's countenance. "Good work! Lily, I don't know what I'd do without——"

But she interrupted in a cool level voice. "I have some more information for you. It will cost you five hundred dollars more—in advance. Fifteen hundred in all. Now."

The smile slowly left Drummond's face; his eyes grew crafty. Then he shook his head. "No, it won't, Lily. I can still tell Brad what you did. Now, what is this business?"

"Penn," she said, with utter loathing, "dealing with crooks like you was a part of my education. Now, unless you meet my price, I can tell you that your precious option will be just so much paper." And as his eyes widened in real alarm, she repeated, "Fifteen hundred dollars, and if you want to pay I have a draft book on the bank."

For a long moment he glared at her, angered and humiliated because she had outmaneuvered him; then, with a low oath, he made a gesture and Lily rose and brought the draft book and pen and ink. Drummond scribbled for a few seconds, handed her the check, and slammed the pen on the table.

"All right, let's have it!"

Lily examined the draft carefully before she folded it. "The farmers are meeting with Embree tomorrow at Stoneman's to arrange for money to help him bid in War Bow Valley." And she added caustically, "I suppose that this will help you ruin them completely."

Drummond sat quite still for some moments, absorbing fully the significance of this news; then, as its importance dawned upon him, he rose, smiling ironically. "You are exactly right, Lily." He stood looking at her, a speculative admiration in his gaze. "What a shame that you and I can't get together!" he said ruefully. "As a team, there'd be no stopping us."

"You have what you want," Lily said icily. She walked over to the door. "Now, get out of here."

Drummond's cheeks reddened. He glared at her for a moment, then slammed his hat on his head and went out.

The door banged shut, but still Lily stood there. She was recalling her promises to Brad, knowing that she would leave Wells soon, but not with him; rather, she would run like the coward she was away from the shame and the pain of things which she had not been brave enough to prevent. Too late, she had found out that it mattered deeply to Lily Farnum what Brad Sutton thought of her.

CHAPTER NINE

Penn Drummond knew that in enlisting the aid of the farmers, Embree had made use of a force which, if not checked, might very well be decisive: either as a potential source of funds for a bid on War Bow Valley or as aroused fighting allies, the farmers would be able to tip the balance in favor of Spanish Spur. Therefore, although he had last night gotten the option from Brad Sutton, there was an uneasiness in him as he went through Wells' afternoon activity toward the bank. The game was drawing too near a close to leave any possible means available whereby Embree might spoil his plans.

Upon entering the bank he nodded to the cashier and moved on through the cool shaded interior to the office of John McVickers, where he rapped once, then, without waiting for an answer, opened and went in.

The faint frown of annoyance left McVickers' florid countenance as he recognized his caller, and he greeted Drummond with the cordiality befitting the bank's most important customer and a member of the Board; afterward, he indicated a chair which Drummond refused with a short shake of his head.

"Thanks, John. No time. Anyhow, what I have to say won't take long. The fact is, I'm expecting Spanish Spur to come to you for a loan to bid in War Bow Valley."

There was an instant, though barely perceptible, change in the banker's face, but he merely nodded, guarding silence.

Drummond went on, "I'll be frank about this: I wouldn't take kindly to a loan to Amy Sutton, John."

McVickers had the grace to blush; but a moment later his eyes wandered away from Drummond's unwavering gaze, and he arched his finger tips into a small tent and considered it a moment before he said, in the dryest of voices, "Of course, she hasn't been in to see me about a loan yet."

"Never mind, she will." Then, having deprived McVickers of this small refuge for his pride, "Those Valley farmers are going to raise a pot to help Spanish Spur, so it's a dead cinch that Amy will be along to you. And I won't have it—you understand, John?"

At this moment, John McVickers was in the unenviable position of disagreeing with the man who was the largest single source of the bank's income, and while he realized that one depositor does not make a bank, nonetheless, knowing Drummond's bullish temper, he wondered if this particular depositor could break one.

He shifted uneasily in his chair, lifted a hand to touch his mustache nervously, and murmured, "I'll keep it in mind if she comes in."

"You'll do more than that. You'll turn her down!"

McVickers' mouth grew a bit tighter and he straightened in his chair. "Perhaps you don't realize it, Penn," he said, managing at once to be both censorious and apologetic, "but the course you're steering lately is not good for the town. You're hell bent on running those farmers out of the country, and if you succeed, every store owner in town loses just so many customers. Have you thought of that?"

"And I could take my account to the Stockmans at Caldwell. Have you thought of that?"

McVickers heaved a hopeless sigh. He had known Drummond would say that but had hoped he wouldn't; now he had, and that ended it.

Drummond witnessed the man's silent capitulation with some satisfaction and then remarked slyly, "Anyhow, you couldn't get a Spanish Spur loan past the Board if you tried. Brad Sutton optioned his share of the ranch to me and I'm putting my beef down on his grass in a day or so. You think Spanish Spur would be a good risk with D Slash cows grazing on half of it?"

He saw shocked surprise on McVickers' face and chuckled. The banker murmured, "Why then, that settles it."

"So it does." Drummond waited a little, letting that thought fix itself in the banker's mind, and then he walked to the door, turned, and asked casually, "By the way, John, doesn't Ed Masters over at the post office have a note with us?"

"Yes—on his house."

"Paid up?"

McVickers hesitated, then admitted uncomfortably, "He's a little overdue, but the interest is current, and he'll get squared away—he's good for it." Then, his gaze narrowing, "Why?"

"Just asking," Drummond replied noncommittally, and went out.

As he headed south along the boardwalk, a vague uneasiness caused by McVickers' criticism of him lingered, and gradually it became a resentful anger which was not lessened by the chilly greeting offered him by two or three tradesmen whom he encountered on his way.

He found Carl Odlum in his office, broodingly paring his nails with his penknife, and after a short greeting, Drummond came directly to the point. "Carl, it just occurs to me that Ed Masters over at the post office will be the one to receive the notices about the auctioning of War Bow Valley when they come. Isn't he married to your sister?"

Odlum stopped working on his nails, slowly closed the knife, and slipped it into his pocket. He glanced bleakly at Drummond and said, "Yes."

"That's fine." Drummond knocked the ash from his cigar; he was watching Odlum carefully. "I could use a little edge on that bid, Carl, just to make sure. If I knew beforehand when the auction was going to take place, and Embree didn't, I'd have that edge." He waited, then added softly, "I want you to see what you can do."

Odlum's face had gone still and frosty. Now he shook his head. "Penn, Ed Masters happens to be a good man—which you probably wouldn't understand. Besides, they've had a hard time since Ed's sickness, and they're just now starting to get back on their feet." He remained still for an interval. "How many good men do you have to ruin before you're satisfied?"

Drummond made an impatient gesture. "What would he have to do? Open the notices, read 'em, pass the word along to you to tell me, and then get sick—go to bed and forget to post the notices until a couple of days before the date. Just enough so Embree couldn't make it to the capital in time. Now, what's so bad about that?"

For a span of moments Odlum sat very still; then he rose out of his chair, his face utterly changed. "You've pushed me far enough, Penn," he said tightly. "I won't touch it—not where my sister's man is concerned. And Ed wouldn't either, even if I tried to make him."

"You're wrong," Drummond said softly. "You will, and he will, too." He moved off the wall where he had been leaning, took a slow step forward, and said with sudden harshness, "If he bucks, I'll see to it that the note on his house is called and the damn place sold. And if you get any funny ideas, Carl, just remember that I elected you and I can get you out of office any time I want to!"

Drummond then saw the rebellion rise in Odlum, and after a moment he saw it leave and saw the hopelessness settle in the man; with that he turned away.

"Penn!"

Drummond turned. Odlum came around the desk, a kind of fright in his eyes. "For God's sake, leave Ed out of this," he begged. "If you will, I'll do anything you want, but those kids are *clean*. Leave them alone."

Drummond studied him without sympathy, and then he said with raw disgust, "Oh, shut up!"

The utter uncaring contempt struck Odlum where he had once been a man. His face grew beet-red and he said, with a soft twisted hate, "You bloodsucker! You've got a lot of us by the short hair, but you'd better hold tight, because this town is turning against you. The storekeepers are on the farmers' side—they want 'em in this country. This thing's changing right under your nose, and I'm glad it is!" He paused, glaring at Drummond. "They're wise to you. They keep askin' me why I don't do something about you."

"Well, why don't you?" Drummond taunted.

The reply which rushed to Odlum's tongue did not come. He seemed slowly to shrink inside himself as he met Drummond's disdainful look, and finally, with a hopeless shrug, he turned away.

"To hell with what people think!" Drummond said harshly. "You just do as I say and forget these day-dreams. You hear me, Carl?"

He waited, but Odlum was staring glumly down at his desk, and presently Drummond went out. On the street he found his horse, mounted, and rode out of town, arriving an hour later at D Slash, where he immediately called Hackett and Taos into conference.

His gunmen watched him stolidly as Drummond paced slowly back and forth before the fireplace, outlining his plans: Taos was to take a crew and move a sizeable herd of D Slash cattle eastward to the newly optioned Spanish Spur range, scattering them as far north as Buffalo Creek.

"And you're to drive all Spanish Spur beef back from the water," Drummond said flatly. "If anyone wants to argue, shoot first and talk later."

Taos got up. "That all?"

"Jump to it," said Drummond, Taos went out.

Drummond then turned to Hackett. "Bob, there's a meeting of Embree and the farmers down at Stoneman's tonight. They think they're going to get together on a bid for War Bow. Only, they're not, because we're going to put the fear of God into those clodhoppers. I want you to get a bunch of the boys lined up to ride down that way, and we'll break up the meeting."

"Good enough," said Hackett unconcernedly.

Drummond paused, his dark gaze thoughtful and narrow. "A good scare will do for the farmers," he said slowly, "but the main thing is Embree. Do you think we can decoy him out of there some way and maybe get him up to Long Reach?"

"Why go to all the trouble?"

"Because people are getting a little leery of us, and Long Reach is a good ways off." He looked at Hackett questioningly. "What do you think?"

"It oughtn't to be so hard."

"Good." Drummond strode the length of the room and back, then stopped in front of the gunman. "There'll be no failure this time, Bob—that's why you and I are going to handle this. Embree's got to be put out of the game for good and all. I won't rest easy until that damned Indian is six feet under!"

Dusk had just thickened into first darkness as Embree, with Tom Houghton who had wanted to accompany him to Stoneman's, rode into the outskirts of Wells, turned into a back street and pushed southward in the direction of Amy's house. Tomorrow, Embree had remembered, was Amy's last day of school for the year, and she had planned to come directly to the ranch for the summer—a move which, after Drummond's night raid of Spanish Spur, he felt would be unwise. Therefore, he had decided to come through Wells on his way to Stoneman's and advise her to remain in town for the time being.

Coming in the darkness to the rear of Amy's house, Embree got down, gave the reins to Houghton, and made his way across the small back yard to the porch, where he knocked. He heard Amy come through the house, saw a light shift its reflection against the pane farther down the porch, and then Amy slipped the latch.

She stared in brief surprise, then said, "Why, Embree! Why didn't you knock at the front?"

"I'm keeping out of Drummond's sight for a while," he said. "Some of his men are probably in the street, and they'd pick me up."

She was still a moment, regarding him, and then she said, "Well, come on in and tell me about it——"

"No time—Houghton's waiting outside." He told her of the new hands he had hired, of the raid on Spanish Spur, and finally of Darby's assurance that at Stoneman's tonight the farmers would raise a share of the bid on War Bow Valley. "I think they mean to come through," he concluded, "because they're up against it. We can live with them and will, and they know that, and they also know what will happen if Drummond gets the Valley."

Amy had listened in sober silence, and now she said, "Let's hope they do. But can't you come in for just a cup of coffee before you go on—Houghton, too?"

"Thanks, but we've got to get along. I mainly wanted to tell you to stay in town a while longer. The ranch is no place for you right now."

Amy cocked her head a little. "Why isn't it?"

"Because Drummond's bunch might come back any time. Hard to tell what they'll do, now they've taken to night riding."

"Oh, pshaw!" Amy said lightly. "Of course I'm coming out. Sam is coming to town tomorrow for me and my things."

All at once, Embree turned sour inside; he paused, feeling an odd anger stir up in him, before he said, with unaccustomed sharpness, "You do as I say and stay in town."

Amy's jaw dropped in surprise, and then her blue eyes flashed and she said indignantly, "Now wait a minute. Is there any reason——"

"Reason enough," Embree said. He was angered because he had spoken as he had. "I'm running Spanish Spur until you tell me to quit. If you come out tomorrow, I'll pack you up and bring you back in. Good night." With a short nod he went down off the porch, and he was halfway across the yard before he heard the soft closing of the door.

Seething with an unreasonable anger and furious at himself, Embree mounted, said to Houghton, "Let's go," and they moved down the street. He was cursing himself for a fool: just the mention of Sam Arnim's name and the fact that he was coming in for Amy had made him act like a jealous schoolboy. Amy had not been to blame, yet he had sulked and been short with her. He had not seen Arnim since the man had sided him against Taos, but in that time a strange thing had happened: Sam had grown able to bring out weaknesses in him that he had not suspected he possessed, and it was a truth that Embree suddenly despised.

And then, all at once he told himself bluntly, Why fool yourself? You hate Sam Arnim's guts, or he couldn't do that to you.

Somehow the admission made him feel better, even while he wanted it otherwise.

They rode into Stoneman's around eight-thirty and put up at the rack between store and warehouse. A number of horses were already hitched there, and Embree heard others moving about in the near darkness as he and Houghton moved toward the store. On the porch, a scattering of men stood gossiping in hushed tones; they peered at Embree and Houghton as they came up the steps, then gave them their greeting.

Stoneman's was a store on one side, where shelves held canned goods, work clothes, hardware, and harness, while directly across the way ran a long bar, the center of the community's social life.

A wide area in the rear was filled with tables, and as Embree and Houghton entered they saw these tables nearly all occupied by the early comers.

In the pale gold light from a rafter-swung lantern, the faces of the assembled farmers appeared sharp and tense, edged with an uneasiness that Embree noted at once; some of them wore guns, and here and there along the wall stood a shotgun or a carbine where its owner had placed it.

A number of the hoemen were ranged at the bar, drinking up a thirst, and after a brief look around Embree moved that way, Houghton following, and a place opened up for them. They ordered, and when their drinks came they sipped them slowly. Presently Sim Darby came forward from the rear and edged up to the wood beside Embree.

"A little early yet," he said. "We'll wait the full time—some of the boys have to come from clear down-valley."

"Sure. What'll you have?"

Darby said to Stoneman, who was waiting, "Make mine a beer."

When Darby had been served, Embree asked him, "How's your girl?"

"Ah," said Darby, bitterly, "if she ever walks again, it'll be with a limp, so the doctor says."

"A shame," Embree sympathized. He placed his elbows on the bar and let his head fall forward a little, and the light shining on the bar top hit his dark eyes and showed them hard, obscure, unreadable; he began to drum on the bar a little with his fingers.

"The shame is that they stand for it," Houghton said disgustedly. "None of this would have happened if these fellows had shown a little backbone."

At that, Darby raised his head. "It's easy to talk, Tom—especially when you're single and no one depends on you for their own life."

Embree nodded. "You're right." He looked up, spied a distiller's calendar behind the bar, and grinned a little to himself; it was a picture of a buxom blonde in pink tights, with a simpering smile, beefy legs, and an hourglass figure, and it struck him with an odd amusement without his quite knowing why.

Houghton saw Embree's glance and followed it, saying with dry humor, "Now, something like that might change a bachelor's mind."

"Or confirm it," Embree drawled laconically, and turned, looking over the room, an unexplainable discontent gnawing at him. The barkeep was in back now, serving drinks from a tray, and Embree observed him and the men before whom he set the drinks : they were taking beer and wine mostly—light cheap drinks, the wassail of temperate men. He decided that there was a significance to that, one that went beneath the surface, reaching clear into a certain concept of the future that such men would make for a country. They opened their snap purses and laid their nickels and dimes frugally on the table and took their drinks slowly while they waited for their change, and always in their minds was a vision of the fructification of one hundred and sixty acres and a future of churches and schools and solid stable towns.

The echo of other riders came on in dull rhythm outside, and after a while new men drifted in. Houghton said, "I'll treat this time," and he and Darby had another drink and Embree passed it up.

Embree was marveling quietly at the fate that had thrown him among these farmers and made him their ally. They were not, he supposed, his kind of people. His kind—the cattlemen, the riders—slapped down their money on the bar and called for drinks for the house; the farmers worried in a stolid patient way about what lay ahead of them and seemed always to be living in a tomorrow that never came. And yet, it would come : Embree had drifted north ahead of it, and barbed wire and smaller ranges lay behind him. These men made a country settle down and tend to its knitting, and the cattlemen groaned about their lost free range and gradually pulled in their horns and began breeding up their stock and eventually made more money out of good beef on less land than they ever had on the open range with its high losses and scrub cattle.

A kind of nostalgia invaded him, even as he admitted that he had learned appreciation of these men; the old way was ending, they were literally plowing it under; but beneath all that the good qualities of these farmers were the same as those of other men, and ten years from now the country would be better because they had come. All the other differences would be as dead as the old Indian troubles, and who would remember a fight for free grass? Or care who had won it, for that matter?

"Better call the boys in." Darby spoke to Houghton and, so saying, raised his voice and called, "All right, everybody in back."

They trooped toward the rear, some of them lining up against the wall, others taking the unoccupied chairs; and the air grew heavy and stale with tobacco smoke and with the smell of sweaty bodies. Embree thought, Now, we'll see ....

At that moment the figure of a newcomer appeared in the doorway. He was a small man, with a hard humorous rashness in his face, his legs were saddle-sprung, and there was a stamp, a mark, about him that immediately sent an alert through Embree. The man looked around the room, small quick eyes taking in everything; his eyes rested thoughtfully on Embree for an instant, and then he said apologetically to Stoneman, "I'm lookin' for Joe Holliday's homestead. You happen to know——"

"Never heard of him." Stoneman advanced toward the door, placed his hand against the stranger's chest, and forced him backwards. "Sorry, friend. We're closed."

The other let himself be pushed toward the door, his face twisting up in a sardonic grin laced with a hidden amusement. "Why, now," he said mockingly, "you're all havin' a party, ain't you?" Then the door closed in his face and those jeering words seemed to linger.

Embree was thinking narrowly that the time, the place, the tone of voice had all been wrong, and he stood tensed, watching the door; then Darby called impatiently, "Come on, Embree, let's get down to business." With that, Embree pushed away from the bar and started toward the rear.

The door's opening caught him in mid-stride; a man had flung it open and now stood there in the dark rectangle, poised and studying the crowd. The man looked at him, said with a sneer, "Good-by, Texas," and then his hand streaked for his gun and he fired.

Embree rolled along the bar as the bullet struck, chunking up splinters. He glimpsed the stranger fading back into the darkness, heard him shout, "Let 'er rip!" and then he saw the farmers rise up and swing into a wild confusion. He shouted at the top of his voice, "Stay put! Hit the floor!" and drew and shot out the lamp in back and pivoted and killed the light behind the bar in the same continuing motion. At the same instant, a full volley crashed in through the windows at back and on the side; a man screamed hoarsely, lost, in the blackness, and afterward his voice sank below the confused shouting.

The place seemed to shake as another blast rocked through the room. Then the rush of the crowd hit Embree and whirled him toward the door, the stampede spinning him around and throwing him into the bar. He drove away from it, a red rage burning through him at this senseless flight, and tore into the pushing howling crowd with knees and elbows and fists as he made for the door with one thought in mind: get at the men outside, find Drummond, who had wrecked his hopes of co-operation with the farmers.

The rush carried them headlong out of the door, and a tight knot of farmers hit the porch and scattered, scrambling over its edge and down its length just as the firing swung around the side of the building. A farmer cursed with helpless wrath and boomed off his shotgun defiantly into the darkness, and over near the door a man yelped, "Stop pushing back there! They've got guns in front, too!"

But the panicky force from the rear was too great, and they piled out and plunged into the saving anonymity of the darkness, hugging its shelter and running silently with the stillness of frightened men.

Embree came to the porch and crouched against the wall beyond the door while the last of them rushed past him; he heard them hit the dirt and scatter and presently he heard no more of them, and he knew it was over. There was some firing from Drummond's men but it was without purpose and the shooting seemed to be into the air. He fired two deliberate shots at the muzzle blasts, from sheer anger and knowing it was no use. The farmers were scattered, cowed, everything but flight forgotten.

He stood up, slipping new shells into the cylinder, and then a low terse voice near him was calling, "Embree. Embree?" He automatically replied, "Here," and a man's dark shape came forward, said quickly, "Thought you'd like to know—Drummond and Hackett headed for Long Reach." And before he could reply, the man was gone.

Embree called sharply, tardily, "Hey! Wait there!" but the shadows had swallowed the man up. He stood listening to the small diminishing sounds of flight, disgust deep through him; he heard the firing stop, and afterward there came to his ears the distant run of horses.

Someone was walking nearby, and he called, "Who's there?" Sim Darby came up, saying quietly, bitterly, "Well, that ends it. After this, you couldn't get a nickel from the whole crowd. Drummond always seems to know what's going to happen before it does."

Embree said nothing; after a while he walked on toward his horse. With his hand on the horn he paused, reflecting, and presently, with his decision made, he pulled up into the leather. That message back there in the darkness was obviously the bait in a trap—and it was pretty crude. But a cold determination had hardened in him, and he pulled his horse around, turned it toward the creek, splashed across it at a run, and headed up into the hills.

Later, he crossed a finger of the Medicines, dropped into a grassy meadow, and sped along it with the night wind stiff and cold in his face, and an hour after that he again climbed the hills and, coming down out of them, hit the Long Reach road and put his horse to it. It was toward midnight when he walked his horse into the town's shabby street.

One dim window of the rooming house put its finger of light into the darkness, and some light still came from the saloon. The silence through the place was ever deepening, and Embree stopped and studied the town for a long space. Then he got down and led his horse toward the skeleton of the blacksmith shop, and there, at a corner of the building, he tied; afterward, he moved cat-footed through the darkness upstreet until the low murmur of voices from the saloon halted him.

Three horses stood at the saloon's rack, and presently he ghosted forward and stepped in between them, feeling for their hip brands. The first was strange, but the next two were D Slash and the hides of these horses were damp and their hair was tufted with drying sweat.

For a moment he stood there, his eyes piercing into the shadows about him, but nothing came from the town and nothing came from the shadows which covered the town, and after this assessment, he loosened his gun in the leather, bent under the tie rail, and entered the saloon.

Three men were playing poker at a back table; all stopped their playing as he came in and looked at him with a dead intentness. Then one got up, shuffled around behind the bar, and set out a bottle and a glass.

Embree was seeing all this, his senses alert to small changes, to slight clues, to suddenly shifted balances; he walked to the bar, poured his drink, and took half of it. Meanwhile, the three men had not moved.

"You want to eat?" the barkeep asked.

"No."

The man shrugged, turned, and banged his fist twice on the partition behind the bar.

"What's that for?" Embree asked quickly.

"For the woman to go to bed. You're not eatin', we'll close up, then."

Embree's eyes narrowed; he stepped quickly to the door leading behind the partition and threw it open. He saw a table with two plates holding the remains of a steak dinner and two cups of coffee still half full. The chairs had been pushed back in a hurry and left, and he noted that and then turned back to the bar. He said softly to the barkeep, "All right, where'd they go, friend?"

"Where'd *who* go?" For only an instant the man's eyes flickered toward the door, then returned to Embree, but he felt the skin on his back tighten and cursed himself for a fool. He reached slowly for the bottle with his left hand, turning his body slightly as he did so, and then there was a soft movement at the door. Suddenly Embree wheeled aside, grabbing for his gun, and the silence split open with a roar as a slug went past him and crashed into the bottles behind the bar.

Embree drove a shot at the door, saw Bob Hackett's thin face twist into a wolfish snarl, then disappear. As he shot out the light Hackett's gun boomed again, and Embree heard the poker players dive for the floor. Outside, the quick run of boots sounded along the boards, and with that, Embree made for the door.

A shape was running in the fore darkness and he fired at it and the breath of a bullet sighed past him in reply. He had his head turned that way, and he whipped around as a sound reached him from upstreet, but he saw no one there. He stood his ground, his lean shoulders flat against the saloon's wall, and then he heard Penn Drummond's voice, quietly exultant, drift down through the darkness. "Come on up, Bob—close in. He's on that wall there, between us."

CHAPTER TEN

FOR SEVERAL MOMENTS after Penn Drummond called down to Hackett, there was complete silence in the darkness. Embree remained dead still, breathing through his mouth so as to lose no faintest sound. Then, down the way, there came the starved echo of a sound—that of cloth rasping faintly against a wooden surface. It came over him that he was a fool to stay here, bracketed by their fire: his headlong anger had drawn him into a whipsaw.

Regretting his rashness, he began moving back toward the door, and presently his outstretched hand felt the outline of the jamb. A moment later, he dodged over the sill and went toward the rear through the complete blackness, saying low and terse, "Make a light in here, and I'll shoot your damned eyes out." In the back he located the door and went through it and found himself in an alley behind the saloon. He paused an instant, listening, then made a crouching run across the back of the building and hauled up at an alley which led to the street.

The sour decaying smell of a refuse heap was in his nostrils, and off in the darkness a rat or other small night animal made a quick scampering sound and then was still. He was staring up through the forward darkness, and after a while he saw a shape move there. He straightened, set one foot forward, testing the footing, and let his weight fall on it easy and slow, and then he tested with the other foot and so moved forward by inches until he could distinguish the blurred shape of Hackett against the lighter darkness. He could almost sense the tight-nerved waiting in the gunman's rigid shape, and after a while he caught the faint sound of Hackett's quick breathing. Then Hackett moved a little, calling in a hoarse whisper, "Drummond?" and Embree heard Drummond, upstreet, softly cursing the man to silence.

Embree sucked in a long slow gust of wind; he eased forward again, letting his breath out in slow pinches; he was fifteen feet from Hackett when some sound alerted the gunman and he whipped around. Embree said, very low, "Here, Hackett!" and saw Hackett's head jerk up. He threw himself to the ground as Hackett's gun pounded and a bullet sucked past his head, and then his own gun, quickanswering, drowned out the other.

Hackett spun full around, hung a moment and then toppled. Embree heard him hit the ground. The next moment the gunman fired again, wide of the mark, and Embree drove to his feet and moved in fast and thumbed off his shot so close that he could see the man's dim shape in the muzzle-blast. Afterward, he heard a faint movement, a long sighing breath, and then no more.

Away on his right, Drummond called nervously, "Get him, Bob?" and the question hung there, shrouded in its own uncertainty. Embree thought with bitter anger, worry about it, damn you! and moved back quickly the way he had come, running easily down the alley, past another house, and cutting down its side to the main street where he paused an instant, believing himself now above Drummond. Then, walking softly, he crossed through the thick darkness to the other side where he put his back against a house and waited, his eyes on the pool of light from the rooming house which lay on the street's dust twenty yards below him.

One thing he knew: Drummond would neither investigate nor long endure this strained uncertainty. The seconds slipped by. Embree's attention fixed on the down-street shadows, and then at the farthest margin of the light he saw Drummond's great bulk backing slowly up this way, half crouched and facing with gun ready the spot where the shooting had occurred. He saw Drummond pause, cast a quick glance to right and left, and with that Embree moved.

He took three long strides and stopped, calling softly, "Drop your gun, Penn, I'm in back of you."

At his words, Drummond froze. For a moment it seemed that he might turn, taking the gamble; then, with a snort of angry disgust, he flung his gun into the darkness, wheeled, and stumped forward a little into the light. A snarl wrinkled Drummond's face and he stood bent a little at the knees, his head lowered bullishly as he glared at Embree.

"Luck, pure damn luck!" he said bitterly. "By God, you ought to buck monte."

"Sure," said Embree, drifting forward and watching the other almost idly. For an interval they stood looking at one another, and then Drummond snarled spitefully, "But you're finished! Tomorrow my stock moves in on you, clear up to Buffalo Creek. And that's the end of Spanish Spur."

"They'll go back," Embree said quietly. "Just like the others did."

"Not this time! They're on your grass legally. Brad Sutton optioned his share to me, and there's not one solitary thing you can do about it."

Embree stood stock still, shocked beyond anger; then he said bluntly, "That's a lie."

"Is it? Wait and see!" Drummond laughed, low and mean. "There's more than one way to skin a cat, Texas, and I've skinned you good. Lily Farnum got that option out of Brad for me, and I didn't turn a finger. Now, what are you going to do?"

It seemed for a moment that Embree did not hear him, but he was thinking of Brad's odd manner lately, thinking of what this would do to Amy. Drummond had taken good men and twisted them and warped them with a complete disregard for human values, and for the moment Embree could see only the harm that had been done to innocent people in this man's uncaring drive for power.

He asked, oddly soft, "Drummond, I wonder if you know that Sim Darby's little girl will likely be a cripple?"

After one surprised moment, Drummond blurted, "So what? Let him get her a crutch. Is it *my* worry?"

"I thought so," Embree replied tonelessly, and let his gun slide back into the leather.

Drummond's reaction was immediate. Embree saw his bullish shape loom suddenly forward, and then a cold rage broke in Embree and he ran forward to meet Drummond's charge.

Embree collided solidly with Drummond, heard the man grunt, and immediately felt Drummond's meaty arms whip around him, trying to encircle him. He drove a right into Drummond's face, and the big man fell back for a moment, then rushed in again, his shoulder hitting Embree in the middle and driving the wind from him. The savagery of this rush carried them back to the hitch-rack, the pole striking Embree just above the kidneys with a deep dull pain, and again Drummond's arms were closing about him and he struggled against them. The next moment the pole splintered and they tumbled to the ground, locked together.

In the fall Embree twisted over and he landed astride Drummond, whose hold had relaxed a little to break the fall. Embree's arm was free, he lashed a right into the man's face and heard him groan, and then Drummond heaved mightily, throwing Embree over backwards.

He lay a moment in the dust, then scrambled to his knees, as Drummond came in once more, silent, his fists flailing. A blow caught Embree on the side of the head, and he went down with a splitting roar in his skull and nausea grabbing at his stomach. Drummond was on him instantly. Embree threw up his arms against the blows and rolled aside; as Drummond came on he drove up his knees, felt them smash into Drummond's face, and the big man let out a low moan and scuttled aside. Embree rose then, feeling the warm flow of blood on his face. In the darkness he could see only the other's huge bulk, and he made a flying tackle and caught Drummond at the knees, bringing him down heavily. He felt Drummond's hand reaching for his throat and lashed out hard with his boots as Drummond came over on him; suddenly Drummond floundered free, pushed to his feet with a curse, and Embree rose up and faced him.

For a span of moments they stood thus, their breathing sounding deep and labored, and then Embree moved in, feinting broadly aside as Drummond reached, and drove a left deep into the man's middle. Drummond's hands dropped, and Embree lashed a chopping blow to the face, and another. For a moment the big man wavered, and then he came on with a straight right to Embree's cheek; the numbing shock of it struck him, and he felt the searing surface pain as the flesh tore. Blindly, he bored in with an uppercut that threw Drummond back, and now they stood and slugged toe to toe.

Embree's arms ached leadenly, the air was thinning in his chest, and he knew that he couldn't go on long this way. Suddenly he broke away and stepped back, and after only a momentary hesitation the big man charged doubled up, all his power driving him forward. Embree stood fast and then stepped aside and drove a down-sweeping blow with all his strength behind it to the base of Drummond's skull; the man uttered a grunt, plowed on past, and lit on his face in the dust, where he lay, moaning softly.

For a brief span Embree gulped air into his lungs, and then he went forward, grasped Drummond's shirt front, and hauled him to his feet. The man's weight was too much for him, and he half dragged him the few paces to an awning post and propped him against it. Drummond was coming out of it; his arms came up, and he muttered something and pulled away a little; then

Embree's blow caught him full on the mouth, and he staggered back. A senseless fury drove Embree's blows in against him, and Drummond merely rolled with them, dumb and shocked, some primitive instinct alone holding him on his feet. Once or twice he grunted with the relentless battering, and then all at once his knees buckled and he fell toward the dust, out cold.

Embree stood staring vacantly at him, and after a while he realized that he was trembling with a killing wrath, that his head was reeling, and the salty taste of blood was in his mouth. A brutelike exhaustion was on him, and it was a long while before reality slowly filtered back to him; then he turned and walked unsteadily down the way toward his horse, stumbling a little as his boots struck the uneven ground.

Long before he arrived in Wells, two hours later, he had lost the reckless momentary satisfaction of beating Drummond into insensibility; the shock of what Brad had done had left him with the weary knowledge that nothing had been accomplished by his fight with the D Slash boss.

Spanish Spur was now split by Brad's action, and even if Amy might care to try to hold on after this, which seemed doubtful, the farmers would be no help and the bank would certainly refuse a loan on a property apparently drifting into complete disruption. He thought these things slowly, glumly, as he rode through the night, and all the while he knew that the worst of all would be telling Amy what Brad had done.

The town was dead, dark and hollow and still, as he rode at a walk down the street, the only sound being the tired ploshing of his horse's hoofs in the deep dust. Before Amy's house he slid wearily from the saddle and tied his horse, and then he stood a while, feeling the lonely cold lift of the wind against his face, feeling its light sting in the cut below his eye. The smell of dust was on the wind, and beneath its odor lay a deep damp sweetness which stirred him strangely, bringing up the lost memory of a voice he had once heard in a mountain town through which he was passing: it had been a woman's voice singing something sad and haunting and sweet, and it had moved him in this same way and he had gone on, never knowing the woman's face nor the name of the song, nor remembering now the town in which he had heard it; and yet its memory had remained, to be stirred to life by a loneliness, a certain sameness of the night wind—he turned and walked toward the house.

For some long moments he stood in the darkness, and when he had rapped three times he saw a light's changing reflection through the window and then he heard Amy's steps and her apprehensive voice asking, "Who is it?"

He replied, and she opened the door, holding up the lamp so that its light fell full on his face. She said no word, but her eyes grew round at the sight of him, and then she drew him in and led him to the kitchen, where she placed the lamp on the table and regarded him.

"What happened, Embree?" she asked, in a hushed voice.

He sank into a chair, saying tiredly, "They broke up the meeting at Stoneman's, and I followed Hackett and Drummond to Long Reach. We tangled—" He shrugged, and a pain in his shoulder made him wince.

She saw that and went from the room, and after a while she came back with bandages and salve, and then she heated water and dressed the cuts on his face. She stood near him the while, and once more he was conscious of her in that deep way, moved by the closeness of her firm young body under the familiar red wrapper. Yet he said nothing, and all the while Amy remained tight-lipped, until she had put the things away and had come to sit down at the table opposite him.

She said then, "I suppose that there will be no help from the farmers after what happened?"

Embree shook his head. "That's done with." He raised his slow sober gaze and looked at her a moment before he said, "Amy, there's worse news than that. Drummond is moving his stock in on us clear up to Buffalo Creek. Brad gave him an option on his share of Spanish Spur."

He saw the color drain slowly out of her face; she was looking at him as though she did not understand, and he knew then that Brad had done this without her knowledge.

She said, very low, "Brad—optioned to *Drummond*?"

"It's a fact that's got to be faced," he said, not looking at her. "If we can't swing a bid on the Valley now, we're cut squarely in half. There'd be very little chance of ever getting Drummond off the grass, once he's on it."

She said nothing but turned her face aside a little, and he saw the bitter tightening of her lips, the discouragement darkening her blue eyes. The knuckles of her hands, folded on the table before her, were white with pressure, he noted. For a long while they sat there silent, the measured ticking of the clock near the stove sounding very loud in the stillness.

At last Amy said hopelessly, "I suppose this means the end, doesn't it?"

He would never tell her how near the end he thought it was at this moment. Instead, he said, "It would be foolish to deny it's bad." He paused a long moment, then added slowly, "It all depends on whether you want to keep going with what's left and try to add War Bow Valley to it. If you got War Bow, Drummond would have to give up his option, and even if he waited to do that just for meanness, War Bow added to your share would cancel out the loss of Brad's share."

Amy waited awhile, thinking that over, and then she raised her gaze to him and shook her head. "But how? War Bow is just a lost dream now—like a lot of others," she said tonelessly.

"You've got to try the bank. We don't know that McVickers will turn down a loan."

She looked at him a long time, her blue eyes searching his face, and at last she said without spirit, "All right. I'll go over this afternoon and see McVickers."

They sat a moment after that, but there was really nothing more to say, and presently Embree rose, reaching for his hat. Amy got up, too.

"Are you going out to the ranch?" she asked.

He shook his head. "I'll stay at the hotel and drop around in the afternoon to see what you've found out from McVickers."

Amy walked to the door with him, both of them silent, and Embree thought it was odd that she had offered no comment on Brad's action. Yet he knew that she was deeply shocked and hurt, and he searched for some consoling word or phrase to comfort her, but without success. As he stepped out upon the porch and turned to bid her good night, the best he could do was to say, "Amy—I can't tell you how sorry I am that Brad did this."

He saw her draw up a little then, holding to her pride and renouncing her disappointment, and she answered in a steady voice, "He had a *right* to do it; that's what I'll think, Embree. As for Dad's wishes—well, we'll keep trying until there's no longer any use to do so."

But as she murmured good night and closed the door, Embree knew that she really did not hope. For that matter, only a stubborn determination not to be whipped kept him from admitting that they had lost. He couldn't see the way out.

After he had put up his horse, he went to the hotel, got a room, climbed the stairs to it, and sank wearily down on the bed, too tired to do anything but pull off his boots and draw a blanket over him. As he fell asleep he had the ironic thought, you won't come out and tell her we're whipped, because if you did Sam Arnim would move right in. What's the difference if he does it now or later?

When Embree awoke, he lay for some moments trying to orient himself. Then he became aware that the noises of the town filled the street outside, and he looked at the angle and quality of the sunlight streaming through the window and got up hurriedly, reaching for his boots. He had slept late into the afternoon.

Hurriedly he washed up, brushed off a part of the grime of last night's fight, then went down to the lobby. As he crossed toward the door, the clerk called, "Message for you, Embree," and handed him an envelope.

Under the clerk's curious appraisal of his battered appearance, he opened the message and read it. It said, "McVickers was sorry—Amy." That, and nothing more.

He remained motionless for some moments, staring at the paper; then he balled it in his fist and tossed it at a wastebasket, afterward turning toward the dining room. There was no hurry now; he might as well eat.

In the empty dining room he dawdled over ham and eggs, smoked two pipes of tobacco, and drank three cups of coffee, all the while thinking with a fierce kind of concentration of what had happened and searching for the way out of the maze. When the waitress began to set the tables for the evening meal, he left the dining room and returned to his room, where he stretched out on his bed, loath to go and face Amy, afraid in an odd way of what her decision might be, now that the bank had turned down their last hope of a loan. It was almost dark, and the shadows had thickened in his room, when he arrived at a long-shot possibility that would either save Spanish Spur or break it. For a long time he lay considering it, reluctant to decide fully because failure meant the certainty that Sam Arnim's dire predictions would be proved correct: Amy would lose everything or nearly so. And yet, he told himself doggedly, she had lost everything now—unless this one chance worked out.

He rose then, his mind made up, and went out into the town, where full darkness had now settled. He went first to the saloon, but Brad was not there, and although he waited some time, he did not put in an appearance; then, cursing himself for a fool for not thinking of it sooner, Embree returned to the hotel, inquired, and found that Brad was registered in room 203. He mounted the stairs, went down the corridor, found the room, and then, without knocking, he pushed open the door and went in.

Brad lay stretched out on the bed, his head pillowed in clasped hands, and he was stone sober. He turned his head and looked at Embree, the thin lamplight showing a tired resignation in his dark face. "So it's you," he murmured. "I've been expecting you."

Embree walked slowly around the bed, Brad's eyes following him, and near the head of the bed he stopped, propped his foot on a chair, and leaned forward a little. "Why have you been expecting me?"

"Stop it, Embree," Brad said wearily. "You think I don't know what I've done—or what it means?"

"Do you?"

Brad fastened his eyes on the wall behind Embree. He said, low and bitter, "All it takes is a little time, and I've had that."

"Then why didn't you let Amy know?"

"Because you'd have jumped down my throat and tried to stop me. And I'm not going to be stopped." He looked straight at Embree. "I warn you, Embree, I'm going to work this thing out by myself. Don't come butting in. After all, it isn't as though I'd made Amy lose anything—she still has her share of Spanish Spur, don't forget that."

Embree nodded. "That's so," he said slowly. "The one you really hurt was your father—he wanted you and Amy to hold together and run the outfit he'd built up. It didn't take you long to show people that his confidence in you was misplaced, did it, Brad?"

A sick look came into Brad's eyes, and he looked away from Embree and let go a long thin sigh. "Ah, Lord! You hit it that time, Embree—that's the thing that keeps me awake nights."

"Then get up out of there and come with me to Lily's. You can tell her to notify Drummond that the whole thing's off—that it was a mistake."

Brad stiffened, his face changing instantly and his gaze coming back sharply to Embree's face. "Didn't I tell you?" he asked resentfully.

Embree murmured, "So you did," and took a quick step forward, gathered Brad's shirt into a ball and hauling him to his feet. He struck Brad a hard flat-hand blow in the face that sent him sprawling back across the bed, where he lay a moment, astonishment and anger burning up in his eyes. Then, with a low exclamation, he came boiling up at Embree.

Embree moved back a little as he came and threw a not-hard blow to Brad's jaw, and Brad stopped short, grunted, and sat down flat, his eyes dazed and vacant.

"Get up and put your hat on," Embree said harshly. "I'm through fooling with you."

Brad shook his head, trying to clear it, and at that moment the door opened and Sam Arnim stepped inside, halted, and stared. "What the—" he began.

Embree cut in, short, impatient. "Get out of here, Sam. No time for you right now."

Resentment glittered in Arnim's eyes. "To hell with you," he said stiffly. "My business is with Brad."

"He's tied up right now," Embree said dryly. "Beat it." Turning his back on Arnim, he walked over to Brad, hauled him to his feet, and clapped his hat on his head, afterward shoving him toward the door.

"March," he said brusquely.

He would have ignored Sam, but the latter stepped aside as they went out the door, saying frostily, "I figured you'd be up to something like this, just because you hate Drummond to hell and back. Brad's his own man, ain't he?"

"It's a question whether he's even a man," Embree retorted, and went on past, herding Brad along the hallway and so down to the lobby and out to the boardwalk. They turned in the darkness down toward the cross street below the hotel and there turned back toward Lily Farnum's house. Brad said then, "Let go of my arm—I'm going with you." And a moment later he said, in a subdued tone, "I guess I had that coming."

Embree glanced at him sharply but said nothing.

Lily opened to Embree's knock. At sight of Embree and Brad together she tensed and her face went white, but immediately she regained her composure and greeted them. "What do you want?"

"We wanted to talk to you, Lily," Embree said.

Slowly she shook her head. "I'm sorry, I have another caller."

"Who?" Brad asked instantly.

She turned to give him a slow strange look, her eyes holding his a moment before she said, in a small voice, "Penn Drummond."

"Then we'll go in," Embree said firmly.

The woman swung toward him and read his face, studying carefully what she saw there. He heard her long resigned sigh, and she turned her eyes for a moment upon Brad before she ansewered.

Then she murmured, "Follow me."

CHAPTER ELEVEN

EMBREE AND BRAD SUTTON followed Lily down the hallway and into the living room, and as they entered, Penn Drummond glared up at them from across the table where he sat. Just inside the door Embree halted, returning Drummond's glare. The woman crossed the room and sank down upon the sofa behind Drummond, her eyes coming back, still and round, to Brad's face.

Drummond was marked by the battle of last night, a black welt smearing over his cheekbone and running up into his right eye, and his mouth cut and swollen. Without taking his eyes from Embree's, he growled, "Lily, why in damnation did you let them in?"

The woman said nothing; pale, she sat with her hands in her lap, watching Brad steadily, and therefore it was Embree who answered Drummond. "Never mind that," he said. "We're here. And we came to put you on notice that we're going to break that option. It'll be easy enough to prove undue influence."

Drummond's eyes narrowed, but he said nothing at once. But he was keyed up, and he was giving Embree's words the full weight of his thoughts. At last he shook his head. "I doubt that," he said heavily. "Lily merely acted as my legal agent."

Brad looked at the woman oddly, then said quickly, "Lily, Embree doesn't speak for me. My plans haven't changed in the least."

A malicious chuckle escaped Drummond. "There you are, Texas," he said to Embree. "What next?"

Embree sent his slow glance around, looking at them all. "All right," he said quietly, "there's no use of this going on. You've got your minds made up, and so have I." He said softly, "Lily," and as she returned his look, he waited a moment, then said with soft startling abruptness, "How much did Drummond pay you to get that option from Brad?"

He was aware of Brad's sudden start, but Lily remained still, a slow hot flush mounting to her cheeks. For a span of seconds he believed that he had misjudged her, and then he saw her eyes change and move to Drummond, all sympathy leaving them as Drummond looked at her and frowned; she swung her head slowly about and faced Brad directly then, murmuring in the faintest of voices, "He gave me one thousand dollars."

The silence held on for a moment, before Drummond snarled, "So what? She had a commission coming. Sutton and I weren't on good terms."

But no one seemed to hear him. Embree's attention was held by Brad and the woman; it was as though Brad slowly shrank inside, a shocked kind of sickness overrunning his face as he stared at Lily. She, in turn, was watching him with numbed indrawn eyes that could be saying nothing or saying anything.

And then Brad's glance left hers and he moved a little and Embree heard his long hard exhalation of breath. "You win, Embree," he said, in a wire-thin voice. "I've made the biggest mistake a man ever made. We'll break the option——"

"Oh no, you won't!" Drummond rose out of his seat, his big face in a tight snarl, his dark eyes a-glitter. "You try that, Sutton," he said, in a tight furious voice, "and I'll tell the world about you."

Brad swung toward him, starting to speak, but Drummond cut him off with a gesture and drove on.

"Who warned us about the meeting at Stoneman's? Who brought us word that your old man was going to cut that herd on the Valley—and got him killed for his trouble? Why, if the farmers ever found out about you, they'd kill you themselves. No, you won't renege on me, because if you do I'll make you a man that this country will turn out—and your own sister will be the first!"

There was an almost breathless stillness in the room. Brad was staring at Drummond, deathly pale. Then, slowly he turned to face Lily, a wounded look in his eyes that brought her to her feet in an involuntary movement toward him.

"Don't believe him, Brad!" she said, low, fiercely. "The fault was mine, not yours. And not even I had any idea that telling Drummond what you said would—would lead to your father's being killed. Brad! Don't look at me like that! You—you've got to believe me...."

Her voice trailed off then, for her words were having no effect on Brad, who seemed to be looking straight through her. Embree saw the defeat and the bitter judgment that came into Lily's eyes then, saw her die a little death in Brad's silence.

Then Brad turned and without a word left the room. Lily again made that sudden futile movement, as though to follow him, and then sank down upon the sofa, hiding her face in her hands.

Embree heard the door open and heard it close, and he turned to Drummond, who still stood scowling at the door through which Brad had gone. "Drummond," he said, with soft contempt, "as men go, you're at the bottom of the heap." He turned and followed Brad outside.

He caught up with him a few yards from the house and matched Brad's pace silently for some distance, and then they turned into the main street near the livery stable. "Brad, look at it this way," Embree said. "What's done is done. You won't forget this for a while, but a little hard work at the ranch will help you to do it."

Brad stopped and stood staring off into the darkness some moments, before he said, low and bitter, "The old man killed, Spanish Spur busted up—the thing he wanted us to save by working together—and I did it all. No, I'm not the man to stay and face that out. Drummond was dead right about me, and that's why I'm heading out of the country."

"But you could make up for it. You've seen your mistake now."

Brad laughed harshly. "You'd think so—but I'd probably do it all over again." He paused, added, "I could never face Amy after this. I'd die first."

Strangely, Embree felt no anger for Brad; he believed that he never would again. He did not forgive what Brad had done, but seeing the price he was paying for it, he could not ask for more. He said, without rancor, "Why in the devil did you do it, Brad?"

Brad's reply was long in coming, and then low and almost inaudible. "Did you ever really love a woman?"

There was nothing Embree could say to that that would sound right. After a long interval, he said only, "I'm honestly sorry for you. You do what you think you have to."

"Yes." Brad started on toward the livery stable, but after a few paces he halted and faced Embree. "Tell Amy she can have it all— what's left. And while it may be a hell of a thing to say now, I wish her luck." He went on into the shadows, walking tiredly. Embree watched him until he disappeared into the livery's archway, and then followed on down the street to Amy's house.

For some moments after Brad and Embree had gone, there was a complete silence in Lily Farnum's living room. Drummond was looking at the woman, who sat staring into space; something in her demeanor made him uneasy, and he covered it by saying harshly, "You made me do that, Lily—you were swinging to his side." And, as she made no move, he added with a quick laugh, "Damned if I don't believe you really hated to lose that boy."

He watched her raise her head and look at him and rise and come toward him. He saw the fury that had turned her hazel eyes almost black and pulled the blood from her face. She was breathing heavily, and she gave him a killing glance, hating him fully.

He stood still, knowing this woman's willfulness, yet all at once surprised at the depth of the anger she showed. She came on, a sudden violence changing her face, and the change stunned him with its intensity. And then she moved quickly and struck him a stinging blow in the face.

He cried out, for it was a blow upon wounds already sore, and then, after an astonished moment, he uttered a curse and dealt her a hard backhand blow that sent her reeling back to fall upon the sofa. She lay there, dazed, making no sound, and he saw the blood on her mouth and laid his oaths against her. And when she said nothing, he picked up his hat and tramped from the room.

Lily heard the door slam shut, but she lay where she had fallen on the sofa, past pain, past feeling; slowly all the hardness that the years had dammed up inside her broke and ran out of her, and she felt the hot tears come. After a long time she murmured, in a low misery-choked voice, "Why didn't Brad hit me? If only he had just struck me or cursed me—just once—I could stand it . . . .

A glum mood was on Embree as Amy opened to his knock and greeted him. As he came in, she told him, "You were still sleeping when I stopped by the hotel, so I left a note. Did you get it?"

"Yes." He shrugged. "It didn't surprise me."

"McVickers was as nice as he could be under the circumstances, but—" Then, in a changed tone, "Come inside. Sam is here."

She led the way down the hall, and as he followed her Embree felt his mood already worsened. He found Arnim standing just beyond the light from a lamp placed on a round-topped center table; the lamplight showed a lingering flush on Arnim's cheeks produced by some argument he had been having with Amy, and his gray eyes were bitter cold as he regarded Embree and said nothing. But there was an on-edge watchfulness about him, and Embree wondered if he had told Amy what had happened in Brad's hotel room.

Amy had paused at one side and was looking at both of them in a deliberate manner; she said slowly, "Embree, Sam has been talking to me again about selling my share of Spanish Spur to him, and I'm wondering if I ought to take the offer. After what's happened, there doesn't seem much chance of holding out. We can't keep going without the Valley now, and there's just no place to get the money for that." She paused, then added, "Sam seems pretty certain that putting my share of Spanish Spur in with his Box A would force Drummond to give up the other part sooner or later, because Drummond wouldn't risk a fight with him. What do you think?"

Arnim said quickly, "I don't see why you can't make up your own mind, Amy. The offer was to you, not to him."

"He's my foreman," Amy replied.

"He may be, but there's no reason for putting a third person between us. You're the one to say yes or no."

But Amy shook her head. "I have my own reasons for wanting his opinion, Sam. You ought to respect them." Then, to Embree, "Tell me: do you think we're whipped?"

Embree's gaze left her face and traveled to Arnim's. Sam's countenance showed a growing stubbornness. His cheek muscles were corded and his mouth lay tight as he watched Embree and heard the latter say, "No, there's still a chance—the last one. Of course, it's up to you to decide, but you don't have to sell to him as a desperation move."

"You're a fine one to give advice!" Arnim retorted irritably. "It happens that I'm not after a 'desperation' purchase. Why don't you tell her the truth—that she can lose everything if she keeps on bucking Drummond?"

"Sam, wait!" Amy's eyes were still on Embree's face. "I want to hear this."

Embree said, "Since Drummond's on Buffalo Creek, you've only got grass and water enough for half your herd—say two thousand head. Why not sell the other half and use the money to bid in War Bow Valley?"

There was a silence, and he saw Amy's expression sharpen, but before she could speak Arnim cut in derisively. "And what good will War Bow be without cows to put on it?" He turned to Amy with a gesture of anger and disgust. "Amy, Brad has already let his share of the ranch go to Drummond. And if you sell half the herd, it'll be your share, because the other is Brad's—by the will. You'll end up with half of Spanish Spur and War Bow Valley joined, maybe, but you won't have a cow of your own on the place!"

She was intent on Sam's words, one small line showing on her forehead as she weighed them. Embree saw the argument make its impression before she turned and asked, "How about that, Embree?"

"That's not so. I'll vouch for Brad's approval—a fifty-fifty split of the herd you ship." Then he added candidly, "I'll admit this is a last-ditch resort, but it'll stop Drummond in his tracks. And herds have a way of growing."

Slowly, Amy nodded. "But what makes you so sure that Brad will agree? He—he's never talked to me."

"He talked to me," Embree said.

"You mean you beat it out of him up there in his hotel room," Arnim growled.

Amy swung around and looked at Arnim, her frown deepening; then she again faced Embree. "Is this true? Did you have a fight with Brad?"

"I gave him a little cuffing to make him talk sense," Embree admitted. Telling Amy what had happened at the hotel and at Lily Farnum's would only hurt her, and would change nothing. He felt a scarring resentment at Sam for having brought this out before Amy, and his anger showed as he looked at Sam.

But the man only said, "If Brad agreed to what you say, he's more the fool."

"Sam, please!" Amy said tiredly, and he relapsed into a glum silence. She stood looking from one to the other and then walked a little apart and stopped with her hand on the round-topped table, staring down almost absently. Presently she turned, her decision made.

"We'll try your plan, Embree," she said. "How soon can you get started?"

"We can begin the gather tomorrow."

Amy nodded. "All right, do that." Then she faced Arnim. "Please try to understand why I'm doing this, Sam. If there's any chance of holding on, I simply have to take it."

He glanced wickedly at Embree, then at her, and shrugged. "I've done all I can," he said resignedly.

"And I appreciate it."

There was a softness, a solicitude, in her voice that rubbed Embree suddenly the wrong way. Now he spoke up. "If that's all the business, I'll get along."

Amy wheeled, surprise in her face. "Why, yes, it is—" she began.

"Then good night." As he started for the door Amy would have gone with him, but he said shortly, "Thanks, no need to bother," and went out alone, without speaking to Arnim, without Arnim's slightest unbending.

Outside, he stood on the porch momentarily, thinking with a dark bitterness, Leave them alone! Three's a crowd—and a damned unpleasant one! and then he moved down the steps and halted, undecided.

Sam Arnim had given in to Amy only because it was expedient, but he had not changed his mind; knowing that, and being aware of the man's unflinching stubbornness, Embree waited, thinking in a cool way that Sam had become almost as much of an enemy of Spanish Spur as Drummond was. Oddly, he liked the feel of that thought in his mind.

The door opened. Embree jerked his head around and moved back a slow pair of paces in the darkness; it seemed to him that Sam and Amy were standing very close together there in the door's half-dark rectangle. He heard the low murmur of their voices. Then the door closed, and Sam came down the steps.

He saw Embree as he came forward, and halted, and for a moment they stood stiffly silent, before Embree said tightly, "Quit bothering her to sell, Arnim. She's having trouble enough as it is."

"She's going to have more if she listens to you," Sam said heatedly. "Why can't you see that?" He took a quick step forward, saying harshly, "What's it got her, following your advice? The ranch split, the bank against her, and Drummond mad as a hornet and ready to take over as soon as he gets the Valley! You wonder why I buck you with her? By God, I always will, because you're wrong!"

"No," said Embree softly, "it's because I'm holding you off Spanish Spur."

For a moment surprise seemed to hold Arnim there, utterly still. Then all at once he moved, swinging a fist, and Embree went below it and drove a blow at Arnim's jaw. It caught him on the shoulder, throwing him off balance, but he pivoted and came forward again, looping a haymaker at Embree's head. Embree stepped into it, parried it with his left, and chopped a right at Arnim's jaw which connected, and Arnim toppled over backard and lit in the dust, his shoulders striking the steps.

He lay there, nursing his jaw, and after a moment Embree said, "You want some more?"

"No," said Arnim slowly, "there's no point in this, though I think I could lick you. I just wanted to know about you, and now I do." He got deliberately to his feet and stood brushing his clothing. In a moment he straightened and looked straight at Embree. "So we both love the same woman," he said softly. "I knew damn well you'd give yourself away sometime."

"We were talking about something else," Embree said coldly.

"Oh, sure!" Sam's voice was thick with sarcasm. "You wouldn't by any chance be afraid that Amy would sell and marry me, would you?"

"Talk sense," said Embree shortly.

"All right, I will. You've been taking a lot of last-gasp gambles with Amy's property, and I've been against you all the way. You ever stop to think that I'm in earnest about it, fellow? Well, by the Lord Harry, I am, because the way things are going, Amy's going to have to sell to somebody—Drummond or me. And if it's to me, at least she won't be broke. You don't think I'm going to get her part of the ranch for nothing, do you?"

"I don't think you're going to get it any way."

"The hell you say!" Arnim replied, in a cold furious voice. "You and your damned suspicions of everybody who doesn't agree with you! Well, they'll do you no good, because it happens that Amy has decided to marry me!"

He stood there then, waiting for Embree to speak, but the silence ran on some moments before Embree replied. "If you're going to marry her, it might be a good idea to remember what *she* wants—to hold Spanish Spur together."

"An idea you sold her," Arnim jeered.

"Wrong again. It was Cal Sutton's wish, and as such, it's still hers. Your marrying her won't make any difference in that. My job is to keep a brand in the Spanish Spur iron, and I'm going to do it. If that displeases you—stay out of my way, Arnim."

He turned and went up the street; he was thinking that he was a fool to let Sam's words hit him this way: he had known from the start that they were going to get married, so why should the mere confirmation now leave him sick and hollowed out, like a man with no insides? Then, out of the blue, it came to him that if he was right in doing the will of Cal Sutton and Amy, Sam was not wrong either—could a man be very far wrong in trying to protect the property of the woman he would marry?

"Suppose he has got some justice on his side," he told himself blackly. "He can never be right for me again, damn him."

And back down the way Sam Arnim was watching Embree go, a jubilance in him that overrode the mild guilt he felt because of the lie he had spoken about Amy's promise to marry him.

He watched Embree stride away, and he was thinking, that took his breath away, even if he didn't let it show! Who the hell does he think he is, anyhow?

CHAPTER TWELVE

FOR THE NEXT THREE DAYS, Embree and his crew worked on the back ranges of Spanish Spur, rounding up small jags of beef and pushing these bunches up into the high meadows where, in three larger areas, he was forming his gather for the trail.

He had made his plans with the expectation that Drummond would try to scatter the drive should he learn of Embree's intentions; and therefore he had decided to ship from Caldwell, some eighty miles down the tracks, rather than from Wells. It was, he supposed an elaborate precaution, but he believed it to be necessary, for upon the successful sale of this herd depended Spanish Spur's last chance for survival. The pastures where he was holding the main herd all had egress from the Medicines through a back-country pass known as Ten Mile, and once they had gotten beyond that point he felt that they would be safe from detection.

Stacey Jennings had answered his call for help with the green hands and would accompany the drive to the railroad. And now, with another two or three days' work, they would be ready to trail out. There remained only one more matter to be concluded: Hodge and Bemis, commission agents at Caldwell, ordinarily handled what spring shipments they could get, but since the number in this case was large, Embree wanted to query the agents beforehand, in order to give them time to establish markets and thus keep prices up.

Accordingly, on the evening of the fourth day after his brush with Sam Arnim and Brad's departure from Wells, Embree rode to town to send a telegram to Caldwell. Arriving in Wells, he left his horse before the hotel and then cruised unhurriedly down to the station; he was just outside the door when he saw that Lily Farnum was at the counter talking to the agent. He paused there, not wishing to embarrass her by his presence after what had occurred the other night, and then he shrugged his scruples off and went in. The agent scribbled a final scrawl on a perforated string of tickets, folded them, and shoved them across the counter. "Any time tomorrow, Miss Farnum," he said. "I'll check 'em straight through to Frisco, and they'll be there long before you arrive." Then he turned his glance to Embree, saying, "Evening, Mr. Embree."

At mention of his name Lily Farnum wheeled, a kind of fright in her eyes; he touched his hat gravely to her, she stared a moment, then wheeled back to the counter, and, brushing the tickets into her bag and briefly thanking the agent, she went past Embree and out into the darkness.

He stood looking after her a moment, then went to the counter and wrote his telegram. He handed it to the agent and asked, "How long for a reply, Charley?"

"Think they can give you a straight yes or no?"

"I think so."

"I can catch Bemis at the hotel, maybe, and I'll ask for a return reply. Suppose you come back in about an hour?"

Embree nodded and started away; then he hesitated. "By the way," he asked, "is Lily Farnum leaving town?"

"Going to Frisco." Then the agent added, "And I hate to see her leave. She's a nice girl, in spite of what you hear now and then."

Embree merely inclined his head and went out the door, saying, "I'll be back, Charley."

Head bowed a little, he walked a few paces on into the darkness, and was surprised suddenly to see Lily Farnum standing before him; he hauled up abruptly, feeling a certain confusion as he muttered, "Good evening, Lily."

She was watching him intently, and in the farthest margin of the station's light he could see a kind of shamed determination on her face. She said haltingly, "I—I wanted to talk to you. Do you mind?"

"Not at all."

She seemed to weigh that briefly for sincerity, and finding it, bent her head over her handbag, took from it a packet of bills, and extended them toward Embree. "I want you to give this money to the farmers—to any families who need it and can best use it." Then, seeing his astonished look, she said swiftly, "It's the money I got from Drummond. Please don't make me say more than that—just take it and do what I ask, if you will."

He took the money. There were a lot of things that he might say, but her eyes were imploring him to say nothing, to ask no questions; and he knew that she had already asked those questions and more of herself, had said all that could be said. He put the money carefully in his shirt pocket and buttoned it. "I'll be glad to," he told her quietly; then he added, "And I hope it helps you."

She started to say something but closed her lips against the words and said only, "Thank you very much. Goodby." She turned away and went up into the town's mingled light and darkness, and he stood watching her, thinking of the strange things that are put in men's hearts.

Lily had one more errand whose accomplishment would be the hardest of all; it was a final debt that had to be paid before she could leave this town, one that could never be fully canceled. As she went north from the station, she was summoning all her will and hardening herself to it; and yet when she mounted the steps to Amy's house her breath quickened and she felt her heart beating faster. But when Amy opened the door, Lily's countenance was composed.

"I have something to say to you," she told Amy, in an almost inaudible voice. "May I come in a moment?"

Amy's surprise showed only in her brief hesitation; then she said, "Yes, of course," and led the way inside. In the living room she turned to face Lily, her face showing neither liking nor dislike. "What did you want?"

"You knew, of course, that I—that your brother has been seeing me?"

"Everyone knows that," Amy replied, matter-of-factly.

A faint flush mounted to Lily's cheeks, and she said in a lower tone, "But everyone does not know that Brad loved me. I wanted you to know that."

Amy's lips parted, her eyes widened a little, and for some seconds she was still. Then, "Why, I—I don't see what that has——"

"Please listen to me," Lily said. She was watching Amy's face carefully, and now she shook her head slightly. "I think I began this wrong. Let me put it another way: do you know why Brad gave Penn Drummond an option on his share of your ranch?"

"No," said Amy distantly.

"Because I begged him to do it. I promised him that with the money he would get from Drummond we would leave here and get married." She paused, her gaze almost defiant; then she went on deliberately, "Everything that Brad has done to harm Spanish Spur was done because I asked him to, or because I used things which he told me innocently to keep Drummond informed. I—Drummond paid me for doing that."

Amy was watching her with a perplexed frown, in which some anger was mingled. She was aware that this confession had cost Lily Farnum something and could not understand why she had made it voluntarily. "Why did you come to tell me this?" she asked in a low voice.

"Because Brad is now suffering for something that is my fault." Lily was looking at Amy steadily, stiffening her will; she went on, her voice flat and toneless. "Brad mentioned to me that you people were going to cut that herd in War Bow Valley. He—he mentioned it only casually, and I told Drummond about it. You know what happened ...." Her voice trailed off, and her glance left Amy's and after a moment came back. "I honestly had no idea that there would be a fight, for Drummond had sworn that he only wanted information to outguess your father." Her voice was low, clogged with pain. "I—I swear that that is the truth. Do you believe me?"

Amy was studying the other girl, shocked, yet judging her words, her tone, her face; she stood there some moments, between judgments, then said, "I don't know, perhaps I do. But that doesn't change——"

"No, I'm not asking for forgiveness," Lily said quickly. "I only want you to know that Brad was not to blame, because he found out that I had told Drummond and—and took the blame for his father's death on himself." She paused, and Amy heard her long sigh. Then in a small voice she repeated, "You have to know that Brad did nothing wrong—that's all." And with that she turned away.

"Wait a moment."

Lily halted. "That's really all there is to it," she said, in a changed tone. "I must go now."

"No," Amy told her firmly. "You owe me more than that, even though you may have meant no harm to my father. But tell me, why do you want to make so certain that I will not blame Brad?"

For a moment they looked at one another, until Lily said, in a bitter tone, "A long time ago I was married to a man who had the power to hurt me, and used it. After that, I believed that all the rest of my life I would be able to hurt men without even feeling anything myself. I—I found out that I was wrong."

"Brad taught you that." It was not a question; it needed no answer. And, as Lily said nothing, Amy added musingly, "And now Brad is hurt by what you have done, thinks that you never loved him——"

"I came here only to let you know that Brad did wrong innocently, if at all," Lily said, with a kind of desperation. "Nothing can be changed between me and Brad now, for he has gone out of the country and I—I'm leaving too." Then, with a thinly veiled irony, "Even if it could, who would want it so? Everyone knows that newly reformed sinners are a joy to the devil."

And before Amy could answer, she went quickly from the room.

At about the time Amy was speaking with Lily Farnum, Taos climbed the hotel's stairs, went to Drummond's room, and pushed the door open without knocking. As he entered, Drummond glanced up from a newspaper spread on the table and growled, "You could knock, couldn't you?"

"But I didn't." Taos eyed Drummond insolently, then said, "I picked up a piece of news down at the station. Embree's shipping two thousand head to Caldwell. You know what that means?"

Drummond stared at him, his face utterly still. "You're crazy!"

"Am I? Then go ask the agent—he told me."

Drummond frowned, and as he remained silent, Taos added, "If he sells that many, he can bid against you on the Valley. Then where are you? Want me to scatter that herd?"

But the other shook his head. "Sit down." For some moments he remained deep in thought, then said slowly, "No, he'll expect that. There's a better way." Quickly he got up, jerked into his coat and picked up his hat, and told Taos, "You hang around here until I get back." Then he left.

Carl Odlum was still in his office when Drummond got there. He opened to Drummond, gave him a short greeting, but neither bade him enter nor moved back from the door.

With characteristic bluntness, Drummond came to the point. "That matter we talked about, Carl. I'm not fooling, and I'm in a hurry. I'll give you until——"

"I've already got it," said Odlum, in a flat tone.

"What is it?" Drummond said impatiently.

"The auction is in a week. Ed'll just forget that he got the notices."

"Good!" A quick excitement glittered in Drummond's eyes. Then, regarding Odlum shrewdly, "This is really worth something, Carl. You won't be sorry, because I'm going to take care of you—Ed, too. Tell him I said so."

"Get out, Drummond," said Odlum wearily. "Just plain get to hell out of here."

Drummond merely frowned, as though the man's resentful words entirely passed him by; he was already planning, had no time to resent Odlum's speech. He muttered, "Sure, sure. Good night," and headed back up the street. Tomorrow, he would draw a draft for forty thousand dollars and have a man on the way to the capital by the afternoon train. Then—he chuckled at the thought—he'd have War Bow Valley in his pocket, and Embree could sell his cows—for what?

Back in his office, Carl Odlum watched Drummond go up the street, a bitter black hate in him as he remembered what he had had to do to his sister and her husband. The manner of Drummond's leave-taking, the calm acceptance of the dishonesty and the pain he had brought, still lingered with Odlum. "Damn him!" he muttered. "Double damn him—he tramps on a man's heart, and by God, he doesn't even notice it!"

Sam Arnim had prowled into town, ridden by a discontent he could not quite name, prodded by a lingering sense of guilt that had remained over these four days since he had clashed with Embree over the course which Amy should steer in the future. In spite of his stubborn feeling that his way would be best for Amy, he had begun to realize that her tenacity in clinging to even the remotest hope of holding on to Spanish Spur indicated a deep-seated wish that he should respect. Embree had made that harshly plain to him; and while he hated to admit it, still the uncomfortable feeling grew that Embree might be serving Amy better than he was.

He had spent some time in the saloon, trying to resolve his doubt over a pair of whiskies, but he got no answer from them; the drink only served to lower him in his own estimation as he admitted the grudging possibility that he could have failed the woman he loved. Finally, plagued beyond his limit, he left the saloon and went toward Amy's house.

He noted the moment that she opened the door that she had been weeping, and he hesitated, then stepped quickly forward, his immediate business forgotten. "Why, Amy! What's the matter?"

She started to speak, then wheeled and walked rapidly into the living room, and he followed, filled with concern.

Amy had been deeply moved by Lily's visit, and the relief of knowing that Brad had not acted through sheer malice had comforted her, even while it altered none of the hard circumstances in which she found herself. She kept thinking of Brad and how he must feel; too, she could not push aside a strange pity for Lily Farnum, who had come to her at the cost of her pride and whose remorse, and the reason for it, was so plain. Brad and the girl loved each other, and yet they had wounded one another in a way that neither would ever forget, and loneliness lay ahead of them. Embree had known all of this, and had kept the hurt of it from her, showing his faithfulness even in his small way: the thought moved her deeply. All at once she had been filled by a feeling of failure and loss. Without fully knowing why she did it, she sank down to the table and buried her head in her hands and cried.

After a long while she heard the knock at the door, and quickly drying her eyes she went and opened it, saw Sam there, and was unable to say anything at all for the rush of emotion that almost choked her.

Now, Sam stood regarding her tenderly, his big face filled with compassion for her misery, and he moved forward, saying gently, "Tell me, Amy, maybe I can help. What is it?"

That kindness was all she needed, and Amy let go, rushed into Sam's friendly arms, and clung to him, wailing desolately, "Oh, Sam, everything is wrong! Brad's gone, Spanish Spur is gone, and—and *everything* is gone."

Perplexed and troubled, he held her in his arms, a little embarrassed by this moment of feminine relief; but he loved this girl and his heart swelled, and after a moment he lowered his head and brushed her hair with his lips. "Go ahead and bawl it out," he said gruffly. "Whatever it is, it'll do you good."

She stayed there against him, and after a while she was still, and she raised her face and dabbed at her eyes, smiling abashedly. "Now, there," she said, moving away. "You see just how giddy women can be. And thanks for the shoulder, Sam, it was a big help."

Her attempt at lightness did not deceive him. He watched her, frowning. "Amy, does it really mean so much to you to keep Spanish Spur together?"

"Yes," she said quietly, "it does."

Sam nodded. The guilty feeling in him deepened, and he found himself regretting that he had done nothing to help her— even though he still thought he was right. But now was no time to speak of it and upset Amy further; it was only later, when he was walking up the street to his horse, that he said, with complete conviction, "Sam Arnim, I guess you've been a clumsy damn fool."

Embree killed time for half an hour in the saloon. When he went back to the street, he saw that the light was on in Larribee's office and crossed the street toward it. At his knock, Larribee bade him enter, and he went in and laid the money Lily had given him on the lawyer's desk. "Juston, here's a job that won't make you a cent," he said. "I want you to pass this money out to the people down the Valley, where it'll do the most good. You mind doing that for me?"

"Why, of course not!" Larribee showed his surprise. "But what—I mean, where the devil will I tell 'em it came from?"

Embree shook his head and turned to the door. With a cryptic smile, he told the lawyer, "You could tell 'em it's a gift from Penn Drummond, but they wouldn't believe you." And as Larribee's jaw dropped, he left, taking with him a different feeling for Lily Farnum.

He recrossed the street to the saloon, seeing Lily Farnum going up the boardwalk on the other side, past him, hurrying into the darkness. For a time he idled at the bar, then went out and mounted and rode down to the station. As he entered, the agent waved a paper at him, and Embree took the telegram and read it. WE CONFIRM TWO THOUSAND HEAD AT TWENTY DOL-LARS AROUND, SPRING RANGE GRADE.

He said, "Thanks, Charley—fast work," went out, and rode back up town, feeling better; then the thing that he had been fighting off took firm hold of him again, and he decided that he owed it to Amy as a relief from her worries to tell her of the con-firmation from Hodge and Bemis.

Before her house he dismounted, standing a moment with his hand on the horn, and found his heart beating up a faster pulse in his temples. Reluctance came over him. It was a lie about the telegram—he just wanted to see Amy. He was still hoping, in spite of what Sam Arnim had told him.

He looked at that from all sides and knew that it was true: Amy had been very little to him a month ago, but in that time she had come to be like a slow drug in his veins, changing him and swaying his judgment and giving him thoughts and vague hopes of a kind that he had once thought were dead in him. She had that power, without even knowing it, to uncover in him things that were unknown to himself, to alter his mind and make him another man. It was so, and he disliked it that way, but now he started toward the house, telling himself that at least he had a logical reason for seeing her.

He came up on the porch at the moment that Amy and Sam moved into the light of the living room, and he stopped and stared and then saw Amy rush to Sam's arms, and presently he saw Sam draw her close and lower his head over her. A coldness hit him in the stomach and he turned away, trembling a little, and walked back to his horse, mounted, and rode out of town.

It was only when he was high in the hills, half way to the camp, that he was able to think of it coolly. Then he told himself, with dry finality: well, you're cured now. Be glad of it. You near made a fool of yourself, and all you got out of it was a good hate.

They trailed the herd out for Caldwell four days later, and it was nine days after that night in Wells that Embree and his men put the point of the drive into the loading corrals at Caldwell. By late afternoon, the bulk of the beef was on the cars, and his job had been finished. Leaving the crew to finish the loading, Embree went with Arnold Hodge to the agent's office, signed a bill of sale, and took payment in cash for the herd. Then he left the office and came back to the street, a gloomy feeling of finality all through him.

For some time he stood motionless near the boardwalk's edge, looking across the station square to the pens beyond the tracks, almost idly eyeing the pall of dust that way, hearing as from a distance the chuffing of the engine shunting cars on the siding, the bawling of cattle, the exasperated shouting of the men, one voice yipping above the clamor, "Get him up there, Houghton! Damn it, kick him in the hocks!"

He had no feeling of satisfaction with the job completed; instead, a gray unrest was in him, one that took him back beyond two years, to before he had known this north country, or Cal Sutton, or—Amy. It was the old unrest that had sent him wandering in the first place, but now it was worse, because he had seen the thing he had been looking for, and it was not for him.

He thought of that without bitterness or self-pity, but with a hot envy of Sam Arnim; then, moved by an idea that bridged all the other changes, he stepped across the dust to the telegraph office. Just before he went in, he had the oddly disconnected thought. You damn fool! She only looked at you once or twice.

Then he went in, and with stubby pencil attached to a string he wrote out his message to Joe Morrissey in Alamogordo. "It's a deal. Arrive in about a month." He would ride, rather than take the train—see some more country, push these things from his mind as he filled it with new sights and sounds and faces.

The agent counted the words, took Embree's money, gave him change, and asked, "Want an answer?"

"This is the answer," Embree said. He went back to the street, and this time tramped with some certainty up to the office of Walker and Walker. Somehow, he felt better; a door had closed, and in time he'd forget even what he had seen behind it.

Willis Walker, the senior partner of the firm which had handled certain of Cal Sutton's legal affairs over the years, greeted Embree cordially. For a time they talked of inconsequentials, and then Embree placed a Manila envelope on Walker's desk.

"Willis, there's forty thousand dollars in this envelope. Count it and give me a receipt."

"A lot of money." Walker smiled. "What's the consideration?"

"I want you to send this money on to your agents in the capital and have them bid in War Bow Valley for Amy Sutton when it comes up for auction."

Walker slowly removed his cigar from his lips, regarding Embree oddly. "You're joking, of course," he said.

"You don't joke about money like this, Willis."

The lawyer's eyes were changing, his face growing serious. He studied Embree a moment longer, then said in an alarmed tone, "Then there's something wrong here! War Bow Valley was sold yesterday—Penn Drummond was high bidder with thirty-eight thousand."

Embree stared uncomprehendingly at the man, and then he smiled. "Now who's fooling?"

"But confound it, man, I'm in dead earnest! The sheriff got the wire yesterday." Then, his glance growing keen. "Didn't you see the notices? They'd have been sent to your postmaster up there for public notification."

"Yes." In a remote corner of his mind, Embree was thinking that at the very last Drummond's dishonesty had won; but closer to the surface was the slow revulsion that came back to him with the memory of faces and words and small twisted acts that all stemmed back to Penn Drummond's use of people for his ends: Cal Sutton dead on his saddle, Meeker lying dead in the mud and rain, a little farm girl who would always walk with crutches, Brad's shocked eyes as he looked at Lily and heard Drummond mock her, Lily's shamed abasement, and now—the end of what Cal and Amy Sutton had wanted.

He thought of these things carefully, in almost miserly fashion, holding each one separately and taking its deep-stirring effect; and at last he was recalling the faith and hope in Amy's eyes as she had said, "If it can be done, I know you will do it."

He rose from his chair, feeling a twisted pleasure because now there was nothing to keep him from killing Penn Drummond. Walker was watching him with some concern. "Do you think there was fraud involved?" he asked Embree.

"That may be the legal term for it."

"Why, then—" Walker began.

But Embree cut in. "Willis, if you had your people in the capital enter a petition charging fraud in the sale, would that stop the transfer of title to Drummond?"

"Of course. But I'll need some facts."

"You'll get them," Embree said, low and hard. "In forty-eight hours you'll have all you want and more." He turned toward the door.

"Wait there!" Walker called, nonplused. "Where are you going?"

"Just get on it, Willis," Embree said quietly. "You'll hear from me." Then he went out to gather his men.

The sun had sunk behind the rim of the Medicine Hills when Embree and his crew rode into the western end of War Bow Valley. Through the gathering dusk they pushed up the Valley as fast as horses, tired after a full day's march, could take them. Around them, as the day died clear and cloudless and burnished-bright, shadows suddenly lay purple-green on the grass, bringing up the evening's coolness and the earth's sweet smell.

It was toward seven o'clock, with the shadows thickening, when they approached a finger of timber thrusting out from the hills' base, and suddenly Embree saw a bunch of horsemen round out of it and pull up sharply.

He reined down a little himself, intently searching the character of the group ahead, and then Houghton, beside him, said, "It's all right—I think it's Darby and some of the Valley men." They spurred forward.

There were a half dozen of them there: Darby, John Deane, and others whom Embree knew only by sight, and as they exchanged greetings, he looked them over: a carbine lay across Deane's pommel, another held a double-barreled Greener tucked under his arm, and Darby himself cradled a heavy Sharps buffalo gun in the crook of his elbow.

"For a minute there," Darby said, "I thought you fellows were Drummond's men. Don't know whether to be glad or sorry."

"Why all the artillery?" Embree asked.

"Strikes me you ought to know," Darby replied dryly. "Mean to tell me you don't know that Drummond bought the Valley?"

"I know that, but what's it got to do with you men?"

"Ah," said Darby softly, "we found out, too. The news wasn't back from the capital an hour before him and his crew came down here and put us on ten days' notice to git—or else." A hard anger was pulling at Darby, and it made his voice curt, as he went on, "Maybe you won't believe it after what happened the last time, but we was on our way to Caldwell to join up with you. In case you had anything in mind, we're six who'd rather fight than run."

There was a finality in his tone that said these men had had the last of it, and Embree believed them. Still, as their due, he explained patiently, "You can do what you want, of course. Drummond won't hold the land legally, because he got it through fraud, but there's no doubt he'll try to hang on with guns, and that's why we're here. When he finds out we've moved in, there'll be a fight." He waited.

Darby nodded his head with weary resignation. "I'm dog-tired of swallowin' my pride and eatin' dirt. If a poor man has to do that all his life, he might's well be dead, I figger. That's why I'm goin' to have a crack at that high and mighty Drummond—with you, or anybody else, or alone. It don't matter. I'm gettin' too old to run, and I'm still too spry to die without clawin' back, just once. I'm with you." He turned and looked at the others. "Did I say it right?"

Embree heard their low growl of assent, and replied, "All right, you're welcome." And so spurred on, his band now grown to a dozen-odd. They rode grim and close-lipped on into the growing darkness, with a slice of moon sailing through thin woolly clouds overhead. Half an hour later a heavy mist had begun to rise from the ground, and by the time they reached the old Post, a thickening fog swirled slowly in the light breeze over the grass and eddied and flowed about the buildings.

They pulled up here and surveyed the ruins. Three walls of the commandant's offices stood, the fourth crumbled to the ground, and the roof was open to the sky. Nearby were the shells of the sutler's store and a warehouse. They dismounted, and

Embree gave orders for them to quarter their horses in the walls of the sutler's store.

When they had done this and returned, Embree told Jennings, "We ought to be able to put up a good fight from the main building here. There's no certainty when Drummond will come, but the main thing is to be ready when he does." He turned and swung up into the saddle, cautioning, "Keep your eyes open, Stacey."

"But," Jennings began, "are you coming back?"

Embree grunted, pulling his horse around. "*Am* I? Just as soon as I can flush Drummond out. You don't think I'd miss this, do you?"

CHAPTER THIRTEEN

A N HOUR AFTER LEAVING War Bow Valley, Embree rode
into Wells and turned his horse downstreet, going past the
saloon, the hotel, the four corners, and on to the courthouse,
where he got down and tied. He stood momentarily motionless,
looking both ways of the street as he tested the darkness, the
lighted areas, the deeper pools of shadow beyond; then he bent
under the tie-up and crossed the walk to the sheriff's office.

A four-day stubble of beard darkened his face, and the trail's
dust and its various untidinesses were over him. As he entered,
Carl Odlum stared at him, and then with a resigned sigh he settled back in his chair, his face and his eyes betraying his knowledge of why Embree was here.

Neither of them spoke for a moment, and then Embree said,
with soft cutting scorn, "What surprises me, Carl, is that you'd
do a thing like that to Ed Masters and Mary—your own sister.
How much did Drummond have on you?"

Resentment flared momentarily in Odlum's eyes, but there
was nothing behind it, no conviction, and it died and his glance
fell glumly to his desk. Embree's face told him that this game was
done, that it would be useless to deny. "Enough," he said, with
quiet despair. "Small things at first, then more, until they looked
big." He hesitated, then asked, "How did you figure it?"

"It had to be Ed, because he was the one to get the notices.
And someone besides Drummond had to get to him. You were
his brother-in-law and you were Drummond's sheriff, so it
figured."

Odlum merely nodded hopelessly. "I just wanted to be sure of the details," Embree said, and started for the door.

"Wait there," Odlum called sharply.

Embree stopped and turned, to find Odlum on his feet, alarm in his eyes. "Where you goin'?" Odlum demanded.

"Send a telegram to the Sutton lawyers."

"About Ed? That he was behind this dirty mess?"

Embree nodded shortly. "It'll have to be him. I can't touch you."

Odlum seemed to think that over; for a long moment he stared at Embree, and then he drew a long breath, unpinned the badge from his vest, and, turning a little, hurled it across the room where it hit with a metallic tinkle. Then he came around his desk and stopped in front of Embree.

"Ed wasn't to blame, you ought to know that," he said in a tight voice. "I put the pressure on him because Drummond said he'd ruin me and call Ed's note at the bank if we didn't play his game." He regarded Embree haggardly, then asked with a quiet desperation, "Can't you say in your wire that I opened those notices while he was sick, and that I've quit now to avoid scandal?"

"You'd have to back it up—take the consequences."

"I'll take 'em."

After a moment, Embree nodded assent and turned toward the door, and Odlum's soft, relieved, "Thanks, Embree," followed him to the street.

He rode down to the telegraph office and got off his telegram to Walker in Caldwell. As he rode back, he knew that Penn Drummond had now lost the legal battle but had not been defeated. No law, no writ, no legal judgment, would ever give the final verdict in this matter.

Then he saw Carl Odlum standing on the boardwalk, waving him down, and he pulled over that way, noticing at once the change in Odlum's face.

"You on the Valley now?" Odlum asked. And as Embree replied affirmatively, the man drew a long breath, looked once around the street as though seeing it in a surprising new way, and then turned back to Embree. "I figured so. I want in this thing, too, if you'll take me."

"You sure about that, Carl?"

"Ah! Am I sure?" Odlum breathed softly. "How would you feel if you'd lost everything, including your good name, and had a chance to get even?"

It occurred to Embree that Odlum had paid for a certain degree of satisfaction and deserved to have it, and he replied, "If you want to do this right, go up to the hotel and tell Drummond to his face that you're finished. And while you're at it, you could mention that we're forted up at the old Post." Then he added, "It might be good for what ails you, Carl."

Odlum's eyes brightened, hardened. He said, quick and short, "Wait for me," wheeled, and strode rapidly up toward the hotel. Arrived there, he went up to Drummond's room and shoved his way in.

Drummond turned from the washstand, scowling, as Odlum entered.

"What the devil do you want, Carl?"

Odlum stood very still, open hate showing on his face. He said with low scalding contempt, "You arrogant fiend! I've just had the satisfaction of telling Jim Embree all about your crooked deal on the Valley." As Drummond's jaw dropped and the shock hit his eyes, Odlum laughed softly. "I liked it, too—but it's going to be more fun yet. Embree's got men out at the old Post to hold the grass, and when you come to put 'em off, I'll be there, lookin' for you. You're whipped, Penn—the Valley won't ever be yours!"

Drummond rushed him. Odlum, feeling wildly good, stepped to meet him and swung all his weight into that one blow. It struck with the sound of a cleaver hitting meat, and Drummond grunted, but Odlum didn't even wait to see where he fell.

He found Embree still waiting before the courthouse. As Odlum came up, Embree asked, "You tell him?"

"He'll be along pretty soon," Odlum said, with a quiet satisfaction. He went to the rack, found his horse, and mounted, pulling up beside Embree. "Let's go to the party," he said.

A Box A puncher had brought the news from town of Drummond's purchase of War Bow Valley, and for two days after hearing of it, Sam Arnim nursed it, wanting to see Amy yet loath to do so. She had left no doubt in his mind at their last meeting that her desire to hold Spanish Spur together was sincere and deep, and as a result his feeling of guilt had grown. He had been working against her all the time, he told himself, and with that admission he found less justification in the fact that he had believed his way to be right: he had been wrong from Amy's point of view, and that was what mattered.

These thoughts had slowly formed into a conviction, and therefore on the evening of the third day he rode to town to see her. As she admitted him, he noted the lines of worry and discouragement on her face, and they did nothing to lighten his feeling of self-condemnation.

It was a subject oddly difficult for him to broach, and for some time they made idle small talk before he came to the point. "Amy, it's only just come to me how you must feel about losing out on the Valley. I honestly didn't know your mind on it." He paused, embarrassed, and said regretfully, "Guess I was too wrapped up in my own ideas about it. I thought you were being a little foolish."

"It's all right, Sam," she said.

But he shook his head, looking down at the table. Presently he raised his shamefaced countenance. "I didn't help you out much in what you wanted. Let's say I maybe even worked against you."

She studied his face a long moment, and then she smiled a tired smile. "You were sincere. That's what I'll remember."

"Ah," he said unhappily, "a man can be sincere and still wrong."

Her eyes seemed to grow softer then as she looked at him, and as he saw that, he took courage to say in a low intent tone, "Amy, give this thing up now. Forget the trouble and the worry. Will you marry me?"

She looked at him for some moments, her blue eyes searching his face with a tenderness that gave him hope; then she reached a hand across the table and touched his arm—a friendly gesture, no more. "Thank you, Sam," she said softly. "I honestly appreciate that, because you've been a good friend. But it will have to stay that way—we shall remain friends. I don't love you."

There was only a small tightening of his lips as she said that. After some moments he said, not hoping, "Maybe not now, but we could have a good life together. I'd try to change if you wanted me to. And maybe someday you could——"

"No, Sam," Amy shook her head slowly. "Never that. A lot, perhaps, but not quite enough—don't you see?"

He sat looking at her, and at last he said in a slow wondering voice, "Why, then—I've been wrong all along."

There was nothing Amy could say, and the silence ran on over a long interval; then Sam reached for his hat and rose, and Amy rose with him and walked with him to the door. As he stepped out on the porch, he turned, saying with soft regret, "I didn't oppose your holding on to Spanish Spur in the hope you'd have to marry me. I want you to believe that."

"I always did, Sam," Amy said softly. "Good night."

He went down the street, walking with head bowed, back toward the center of the town. He was reflecting that the only justification he had had for his past actions, really, was the belief that sometime Amy would marry him, and that thus he would be offering her a double safety from Drummond's threat. He had underrated her determination and misread her real wishes, and in so doing he had performed a disservice for her—he might have helped, had he not been stubborn and blind. And then all at once he thought of Embree, and a dark resentment against the tall Texan came through him. He thought, and in the end, he was wrong, too! Let's see him save Spanish Spur now!

He mounted and turned his horse out of town, and as he came to the four corners he saw with some surprise Embree and Carl Odlum riding toward him. They spied him in the same instant, and as they came abreast he reined in his horse and they stopped.

He gave Odlum a short nod, and then he turned to Embree. "I've got something to say to you, just to clear the record. In case you may have a different impression, it galls me, too, that Drummond has beaten out Spanish Spur—but only because of Amy."

Embree said dryly, "It doesn't matter to me what you think about it, Arnim. But the fact is, Drummond hasn't licked us yet."

"Ah," said Sam, "still the iron man!"

Odlum interrupted. "Drummond hasn't got title because there was fraud in the sale. He'll try to buy the grass some other way, though, and Embree here has a bunch out at the old Post waiting for him. If you're so damn sorry, you can save your tears."

Arnim digested that, then turned to Embree. "Is that a fact?"

Embree merely nodded.

Then here's my chance to prove what I just told Amy, Arnim thought. Aloud, he asked, "You headed for there now?"

"Yes."

"Then I'm going, too."

Without invitation, he wheeled his horse and fell in with them, and Embree, saying nothing, booted his horse on up the street; he was thinking that it had taken Arnim long enough to get on the right side of the fence.

On the outskirts of town they spurred to a run and held a fast pace all the way back to War Bow Valley. They identified themselves and rode in, and after the first surprise as the men recognized Arnim and Odlum, they settled down to wait for Drummond's coming....

It was ghostly quiet, with the fog weaving its slow pattern against the darkness, the silence broken only by the occasional stomping of horses, the muttered snatches of conversation among the men. Embree stood peering over the adobe ledge of a window toward the forward darkness, the slow inevitability of what was coming crawling along his nerves, tightening them.

It was toward eleven o'clock when he heard the drumming of running horses, and as he jerked to an alert the sound grew out there beyond the wall of mist.

He sang out, "Rouse up—they're coming," and heard the men stir up to readiness.

The mist had thickened, giving the Valley an eerie appearance. Overhead, the stars were clear and frosty-bright, and a slice of moon rode farther down the sky, remote, lightless. Off in the shifting whiteness rose the steady rhythm of horses moving at a run, slowing to a walk. Then the shapeless outlines of riders appeared at the farthest margin of Embree's vision, and he knew that Drummond was approaching. John Deane ghosted up, rested his carbine on the window ledge, and said nothing. Chuck and Houghton moved silently past toward a waist-high break in the wall. All were straining their nerves against the slowly eddying fog above the grass.

Drummond's crew showed as a widely dispersed ring of shadows fifty yards away. Drummond's hard voice, sounding clear on the heavy air, rose at them.

"Embree, I'm coming in and run you off my land!"

Embree said, "It's not your land and it never will be."

There was no certainty about it, but Embree surmised that Drummond had a couple of dozen riders with him: his own crew and the Long Reach outlaws.

Drummond shouted, "You farmers hear me? This is your last chance. Drop your guns and come out with your hands up, and you'll save your hides."

"They can't hear that kind of talk," Embree mocked.

There was a small silence. Drummond said with finality, "All right, we're moving in."

Embree called, "You lost this deal by a crooked play. It's still public land. Stay back there, Drummond."

"There was an auction and I bought it. I intend to hold it."

"I've stopped transfer of title to you," Embree replied, harsh and deliberate. "You won't even get another chance to bid—but Spanish Spur will. Now, get off this grass!"

Drummond's reply was wrathy, wild. "You damned Indian! I'll prove you wrong here and now!"

"All right, Drummond," Embree's voice was flat in the darkness. "The talk's over. Cut loose your wolf."

Then he heard Drummond say, short and sharp, "Move in, boys. Blast 'em out of there."

CHAPTER FOURTEEN

I N A WEEK of aimless wandering through the hills, Brad Sutton had learned that flight was not the whole answer. His first blind headlong rush into the lost country north of the Medicines had been blunted by the slow realization that he could not leave behind the things which had driven him from Wells, for they rode with him, and when he arrived at any camp, in whatever place, he found them waiting there.

The remembrance of Lily's duplicity remained like an unhealed wound inside him, and yet he knew that deep inside him he only wanted and needed her more. It was this admission which set him to recalling all the small extenuating circumstances which might hold some justification for her: her admission of guilt, her attempt to take the blame to save him from self reproach. How could she have done that if she had not cared for him?

He lived with these thoughts as he wove his whimsical trail over the hills, unable either to straighten that trail out into full flight or to retrace it. Remorse at having treated Amy badly, at having disregarded his father's will held him there: shame was like a poison in him when he thought of it.

Yet, almost without his knowing it, his pattern of travel began to define a slow half-circle which drew back toward Wells yet remained distant from it; he was ridden with indecision, and in this state he came one evening toward nightfall out upon the brow of a hill above the railroad midway between Wells and Caldwell. He stopped his horse and looked down upon the switch and water tank at stop 8, where a siding and a telegrapher's hut indicated the importance of the place. Smoking an idle cigarette, Brad sat for some minutes, trying to think into the future. As he watched, the light in the small station came on, and moments later he heard the distant lonely wail of the westbound mixed freight-and-passenger, which twice weekly came through Wells in the late afternoon. The sound further provoked his discontent: he was tired of this wandering without aim, he was hungry, and he was getting no place—he needed a town, and people, and new sights to get his mind out of the gloomy rut into which it was settling. So thinking, he put his horse down the slope, and some moments later rode up to the station and dismounted.

The agent raised a surprised countenance as Brad entered, but Brad's words reassured him. "This is no stick-up. Does that train stop here?"

"Five minutes for water," said the agent. "You figurin' on catchin' it?"

Brad said, in answer, "Look, I'll take ten dollars for the horse. Want to buy him?"

The agent got up and went to peer through the window at Brad's horse, then turned with a crafty look. "How do I know he wasn't stolen?"

"You don't. If you did, the price would be forty."

The man shrugged, took out a wallet, and counted out the money. The train's two sharp hoots sounded down the tracks, and the agent said, "You'll find a sack in the tool shed for your gear." Then he picked up a lantern, lit it, and went out. The train's hiss and rumble were closer now.

Brad stripped off the saddle and bridle, sacked it, and tied the horse with a rope halter to a corner of the tool shed. The train had stopped with a screeching and a sighing of escaping steam. Brad swung the sack over his shoulder and went down the track toward the lighted windows of the passenger car behind the baggage coach.

Boots crunching into the cinders, the brakeman trotted past him, saying, "Only one passenger coach today—you'll be lucky to find a seat. Better hold on to that saddle." He went on toward the engine, where the train crew was gossiping while the water tanks were being filled.

Brad swung his saddle up to the platform, went up behind it, and paused, peering through the sooty window into the coach. In the dim light from the two overhead reflector lamps, he could see that all seats were taken. He kicked his saddle to one side and sat down on it wearily, and a moment later the whistle shrilled a blast and the train jerked and began to move. As it gathered speed, the conductor swung up on the steps, paused on the platform and looked at Brad.

He said, blowing out the lantern, "Better move inside unless you've got a stomach for soot and an eye for cinders, cowboy. There's one seat free—up front."

Brad got up without reply and followed the conductor into the car. The man went ahead, lowering the lamps and throwing deeper shadows into the coach. As he reached the front he waved an arm at Brad and disappeared into the baggage car. Brad went down the aisle, saw a woman huddled into the corner of a seat, apparently asleep, gave her only a quick glance, and sat down, turning his face straight ahead and thinking, all at once, that this move solved nothing either.

And then a thought rising out of his subconscious came back to hit him hard, and he turned and looked closely at the woman on the seat beside him, his heart suddenly pounding . . . .

For some moments he sat rigid, and then he leaned over and touched her arm, saying unsteadily, "Lily."

She stirred, and he spoke again, and then she stiffened and turned, her eyes wide and startled. For a long moment they merely looked at one another, and then her eyes melted and she leaned toward him, saying very low, "Thank God! Nothing's happened to you. Oh, Brad, Brad! I've been so miserable!" He took her in his arms and held her tight, a lump in his throat choking back his words.

A long time later, when the conductor came out of the baggage car, he looked twice at the man and the woman on the front seat, thinking wryly that it hadn't taken that young fellow long to get acquainted; and then the woman saw him and spoke to the young man and the latter turned and said to the conductor, "When we get to Caldwell, you can have 'em put this lady's bags off. She's changed her mind—not going to Frisco."

The conductor shrugged, said, "It's a free country," and went back through the car past the passengers who were trying to doze.

Brad looked at Lily with complete happiness in his face, and murmured, "In fact, she's not going any place, any more than I am. We're both going back and face it—together. Right, Lily?"

Lily merely nodded, her eyes shining, and moved closer.

A swift excitement shot along Embree's nerves as he heard Drummond order his men into the fight. He heard the horses moving through the night, whose deepening mist gave to everything an indefinite changing shape. Waiting, his gun over the window's ledge, he felt a breeze lift up coldly and saw it swirl the mist and saw the whiteness roll down on the buildings. In back of him someone grumbled disgustedly, "Can't see a thing!"

Drummond's crew drifted in with the fog, and abruptly Drummond's voice rose. "Smoke 'em out!" There was a drumming burst of hoofs, their shapes emerged from the fog, and a roll of gunfire snarled up, sudden and abrupt; then, as the orange flame stabbed the shadows, Darby's buffalo gun began to boom its heavy echoes.

Embree saw a rider dart from the mist, raise his gun, and fire twice; Embree shot at him, heard a sharp cry and a curse, saw the horse wheel and lunge back into the soupy darkness. Beside him, John Deane was levering his carbine steadily, its medium voice pounding with angry regularity. Out in the darkness there was a shifting, a confusion, while within the adobe the firing had settled into a steady cadence.

A man howled angrily from the blackness, "Drummond, you can have this!" Embree, watching for a target, saw a pair of riders sweep in, making a wide run across the front of the building and firing as they came. Then, all at once, all of Drummond's men began to circle the adobe, weaving their horses in and out of the fog. Lead splattered and chinked into the adobe, and behind Embree someone grunted hard, then let out a long pain-filled "Ah-h-h-h."

Toward the south wall a Drummond man suddenly yipped, "Hey! They're open down this way!" Instantly two men raced their horses in, their guns pounding. Embree wheeled, calling, "Somebody over here!"

Morg Tate replied, "Right with you," and raised his gun and fired twice at the shapes disappearing into the fog. As the two moved out, another plunged straight in on a tall horse, his gun blazing. Embree rose before him and drove in his shot, and the horse shied away. The man fired as it wheeled, and Embree heard the bullet hit. Embree laid his fire on this man once more and the horse screamed, bucked, and sank to the ground, and the rider left the leather and hit the earth ten feet away. He seemed to flatten into the ground, and then his gun blasted and lead screamed past Embree. Embree spotted the man scuttling away and hit him with his next bullet, and then a riderless horse pounded by and Embree saw the man no more.

He turned, calling, "Morg—Morg—?" and heard a sigh almost at his feet. He bent and raised Tate's upper body, felt the free flow of blood into his hand, and suddenly Tate went limp. Embree pulled his body over near the window and left him.

It then seemed to him that they tried to rush the door, for there was a sharp vicious dogfight over there. Odlum shouted, "They're down, sneakin' along the wall! Watch out!"

Embree made for the window, and as he hit the ground outside he heard Deane follow. He rounded a corner of the building in fog, feeling Deane close by him, and then saw a flash up near the doorway and blasted at it. Shots rocked the darkness over to his right. The shadows covered everything, the mist eddied and swirled, and everybody was reckless and full of his own angry juices. Darby's Sharps kept booming at regular intervals, relentless, unforgiving.

Embree heard the quick trip of steps coming toward him, and a man loomed out of the fog, jerked around, and fired wildly. Beside Embree Deane's carbine spoke, and the man hesitated a surprised instant, then sank down to the earth. The doorway was clear now and his men held to their cover and poured in a merciless fire, while Drummond's crew, the edge of their headlong attack blunted, held to their saddles and circled through the mist, searching for a weakness in the defense. A horse rounded the corner and came at Embree, and he backed against the wall as the animal loomed above him. Sensing his presence it sheered off, and Embree threw a shot at the rider, who held low in the saddle, avoiding the bullet, and spurred on into the darkness.

Suddenly, as quickly as it had come, the attack broke off. Embree could hear Drummond's horsemen veering off into the darkness. Deane swore after them, and Darby's gun gave a final "Whoom!"

Drummond's voice laid a whipping wrath on his crowd. Embree's men began filtering from the adobe, and he warned, "Stay back there! This isn't over yet."

In silence they waited. Powder smoke settled about them, thick and acrid, and Embree felt the cold shifting of the wind on his face; out ahead he saw the fog lift and part and whirl away for an instant, and behind it the low-running shapes of men.

"They're after the horses!" He started running, others with him. Darby's gun bellowed, and with that the firing growled up again. Those with him answered the fire, and back at the adobe they were potting off toward Drummond's horses.

All at once he was at the wall of the sutler's store, and firing was all around him. A man yelped, "Hold your fire, you fools! We'll kill each other!" Drummond's men came in with a rush. Embree was caught in the middle of it, colliding with first one, then another, and lashing out with his fists both times. They were all mixed up and milling, each afraid to fire and afraid of being fired upon. Back a way he heard Sam Arnim swearing, loud, and an unrecognizable voice blurted scathingly, "No, damn it! I'm Spanish Spur." A hard-flung arm struck Embree in the mouth and he reeled back and reached and found nothing, and the next moment a man shouted, in a voice reeking with disgust, "This won't work. To hell with it!" Then they were running through the darkness, fast-fading targets. A gun spat beside Embree, one of the running shapes tripped and fell, and man cried in a fearful voice, "Hey, wait! Help me." The rest of Drummond's bunch rushed out into the distant haze, and someone back among the horses said, "Well, they're all here—we stopped that."

There was a little firing up by the adobe. Darby's heavy gun let out its sullen growl once more, and a six gun barked, and then Embree heard the angry argumentative talk out beyond the soft wall of mist. Presently there came a shifting about of horses, the straining of leather and the jingle of metal. Afterward he heard the sudden pounding of hoofs roll away and die.

Standing there, slack and tired, Embree knew that it was over for now. Drummond's crew had quit, and while he might try again, it would be no use; his power in this country had been broken.

Houghton went over to the man on the ground, struck a match, and had a look. He came back, and Embree asked abstractedly, "Who was it?" and Houghton merely shrugged. Embree turned away, and the others trailed after him toward the adobe. A group of them were clustered in the shadows, and as Embree came up, Jennings turned, saying, "Embree, it's Sam Arnim—dead."

He said nothing, for the quick feeling that hit him could not be voiced. After some moments the others went away to search for other casualties, and Embree knelt and lit a match and looked down at Arnim. There was a very neat hole, with only a little blood, high on Sam's shirt front.

He was held in an odd suspension between two judgments, where he let himself feel no emotion; and then, suddenly, he was glad that Sam Arnim was dead, because he could hope again——

At that instant, Sam moved.

He did not want to believe it, but even as the match burned his fingers and he dropped it and the darkness came back, his mind told him that the slow small lifting of Sam's chest had been unmistakable. But Sam couldn't live until a doctor was brought, he told himself; he couldn't survive a ride to town supported by someone in the saddle over the rough trails of the Medicines; they all thought him dead, and when morning came and they looked after bodies, Sam would be long gone and no one would ever know. It was easy, in the darkness like this, to think that a man had moved, when he had not: Sam was really dead—he had to be.

Then light another match and make sure, an inner voice prompted him.

He waited a long while, fighting that, and then he reached over, found Sam's wrist, felt for the pulse, and presently found it—weak and fading. There was no doubt. He dropped the wrist and rose, his heart beating up a faster tempo in his temples as he walked away.

And then, without wanting to, he stopped in his tracks. Suddenly, he knew a strange thing: he knew that every man has two lives, and the second one is a secret one from the world and from a man's own self; it is a life which begins when a man has found out the worst that is in him. His had begun when he had

let himself be swayed by Amy's sweet tenderness and her desir-
ability, and from that point on he had discovered in himself the
dark resources to help him envy Sam, and then hate him, and
now to wish him dead because with Sam out of the way he could
breathe life into his own lost hopes.

As Embree stood there, looking both ways from this
moment, he saw that in the past there had really been nothing
in Amy's demeanor toward him that had warranted his hoping. And now, seeing into the future clearly, he knew that he
could neither face Amy nor himself nor other men if he let Sam
die—Sam, who once had saved his life, for whatever strange
reason.

A hot wave of shame and self-disgust hit him, and suddenly
he wheeled into the darkness, cursing himself, cursing Sam. As
he ran toward the horses, he lifted his urgent shout. "Somebody
give me a hand! Sam's still alive, and I'm taking him in to the
doctor."

Doctor Noble looked up from the surgical table where Sam
Arnim lay, where Embree had helped the doctor probe for the
bullet. Sam was breathing very slowly, very shallowly, and as the
doctor regarded him with professional concern, he slowly shook
his head.

"He might live," he said dubiously. "He's lost a lot of blood,
and he has a punctured lung, which means danger of pneumo-
nia. If he pulls through, he's got you to thank."

Embree remained silent a moment longer, then moved to
the door, where he turned and looked at the doctor. "No, he can
thank Amy Sutton," he said, with a shake of his head. "He's her
worry now, and I'd advise you to send for her."

The doctor said, "Probably best. He'll need nursing, and I
only have the Mexican woman."

As Embree said good night and left, he heard the medico telling the woman to bring Amy, and he was pulling up into the

saddle when the Mexican woman came from the house, a shawl about her head, and hurried away toward Amy's house.

Embree reined the other way and rode straight up the middle of the street toward the hotel, where he got down. He stood there a moment in the dust, his long mouth soberly drawn, his dark eyes reflective. The sweep of air through the street's funnel brushed his face, freshening in his nostrils. He was thinking, what now? and deciding that his job was done: Drummond would never get Spanish Spur and the farmers off the Valley now. The rest of it, he had better not think about any more. He turned, crossed the dust to the saloon, and went inside.

At that moment, Penn Drummond and Taos entered the town's north end, saw Embree crossing the street, and pulled up. They talked low for a moment, and then Taos drifted his horse aside into the shadows and got out of the saddle.

Drummond rode on down the street, his square face showing hard and implacable in the occasional light which cut across it. By the hotel he pulled up, raised his head and stared at Embree's horse, and then edged his own into the rack, dismounted, and tied. He shifted his gun belt a little, took a long look across at the saloon, and moved out to the street's middle, where he tramped purposefully up the way to the General Mercantile. There, he put the small of his back against the tie-up and waited.

The Mexican woman delivered the doctor's message, and Amy grabbed up her light coat and followed the woman out, hastening up toward the doctor's house. She had not gone twenty paces when she saw the figure of a man crossing the street above and recognized Jim Embree. She slowed her pace, frowning, for she had thought him still in Caldwell. And at the same moment she heard a horse coming on behind her, and she turned her head and saw Penn Drummond ride slowly into the light. He passed her, and she stood pondering this as Drummond stopped before the hotel and dismounted. Then she saw him move north in the street and lose himself in the shadows. Making nothing of it, Amy went on, but what she had seen puzzled and worried her.

Doctor Noble let her in and took her to Sam, and there he told her in a low tone of what had happened at War Bow Valley. As he spoke, he saw Amy growing tense, and when he had finished, her eyes were wide with alarm.

"Then Drummond took a licking out there?" she asked.

"From what I could gather. That Embree of yours doesn't talk too much."

Amy was thinking of what she had seen in the street: Embree crossing casually, unsuspecting, to the saloon, and Drummond, who had just been whipped, noting this and slinking away into the shadows above the saloon.

She said suddenly, "Doctor, do you have a gun?"

"Why, yes," he began, surprised.

"Then give it to me. And hurry! There isn't much time."

The saloon was deserted, the barkeep readying to close. Embree had a slow drink, bought some bread and smoked meat and a couple of cans of beans that the barkeep rustled up in back, and then, paying for them, he tucked the paper bag of supplies under his arm and went out.

On the boardwalk he paused momentarily, pulling the air into his lungs and feeling the warmth of the whiskey work its way along his veins from his belly. Then he stepped down into the dust and started across the street.

"Embree!"

He knew who it was even as he jerked around. His glance, racing through the upstreet shadows, found Drummond's great bulk, and slowly he let go the package under his arm. As it fell a strange fierce exhilaration ran through him.

Without really knowing it, he had felt all along that it would end this way, and now it was here, and it pleased him in a gray chill way. Slowly, on balance, he squared around facing Drummond and waited.

They stood perhaps thirty feet apart. Embree said, soft and low, "Any time, Drummond."

Drummond's implacable hate had spoken for him until now, but with these words his hard waiting broke and he took a lurching step forward, drawing his gun.

Embree drew and fired. He saw Drummond's gun kick back his wrist and saw the barrel steady again; he saw Drummond come on. The roar of the shots rolled through the street, and somewhere boots were hitting along the boardwalk and a lighter sound of rapid running was in the night. These sensations hit Embree as one, and a bullet snarled past him and the smell of powder was in his nostrils.

He did not fire again, although Drummond's gun was settling into position: he had heard his first bullet slap into Drummond, heard Drummond's breath leave him in a hard grunt. The big man's gun came down, his stride caught, and as he fell his gun rocked the night again and the slug blew up dirt wide of Embree and sang off into the darkness. Drummond fell forward on his face, skidding a little as he hit, and then lay still, a dark stain of shadow on the lighter dust.

Someone was running down the way. Embree was conscious of movement before the hotel but paid no attention. Slowly he holstered his gun and walked toward Drummond's body, and then all at once as he almost reached it, the noises were sucked out of the street again, leaving a taut silence.

It was the stillness, so sudden, so complete, that warned Embree.

He threw his head up and his glance ran a full halfcircle of the forward darkness, and he saw Taos moving catlike down through the shadows toward him, his thin sharp face a mask of hate above the barrel of the gun in his hand.

Then Taos stopped, and his voice came as a hard-hating whisper. "Payoff, Embree. You've slapped your last man. Draw your gun."

Embree had time to think bleakly, why didn't I figure this? and then his hand streaked for his holster. Even as he reached, he knew that it was too late, for Taos' gun had come up and steadied. Embree saw the flame, heard the bursting roar, and then he felt a jolt like a great weight slamming into him. Just as the lights went out it seemed that there was another shot off to his right, but it could have been an echo, for all his senses had exploded.

Then he heard and knew nothing.

CHAPTER FIFTEEN

WHEN EMBREE BECAME CONSCIOUS, it was first merely an aching awareness of a dull black pain all through his head which gradually sharpened as his senses came alive. He lay a long while getting used to it, thinking, Taos must have shot me in the head. How the devil can a man live with a bullet in his brain?

Then he opened his eyes. He was lying in a bed in a room which at first appeared strange, and which he then recognized : it was in the Suttons' house in town. The curtains were swaying a little in the breeze, and the breeze's warmth told him that it was afternoon. He pondered that as an important discovery, and then he slowly turned his head on the pillow, feeling the bandage on his head for the first time.

Amy stood nearby, and at her side was Doctor Noble, regarding him with a professional interest.

"How do you feel?" the doctor asked.

"Headache as big as this room. Weak as a kitten."

The doctor nodded. "You've been unconscious for five days— concussion. Lucky it was no worse. Another day and you'll feel stronger, and maybe I'll let you get up. That bullet rapped your skull pretty hard."

Embree nodded his head a little, and the doctor left. For a moment after that Embree stared at the door, and then he turned his eyes to Amy.

"How's Sam?"

"He's going to be all right." She pulled a chair forward and sat down near the head of the bed, watching him with large sober eyes that now had that deep violet color. She said, "Out there in the street where you met Drummond there was a package of food you'd dropped. Were you going away, Jim?"

It seemed odd to hear her call him Jim. He made a slight gesture. "The Valley was safe, and I'd wired Joe Morrissey I'd be along to Alamogordo. That horse ranch looks like a good thing."

She looked down at her hands in her lap, saying nothing for a moment. When she spoke, it was in a very quiet voice. "I've found out a lot of things since you were hurt—about Lily and Brad, that you knew about them and didn't tell me, that you let Brad leave, and why. Things you didn't want to tell me...." Her voice trailed off.

"No reason why I should have," he said.

She seemed to be thinking of something that was hard to say. "Brad and Lily came back—together. They're going to get married, and I'm glad of it." Her eyes came up, searching his face. "I think I'm going to like her, after what she's told me." A pause; then, "Do you believe that—well, caring for someone the way she and Brad do can change people?"

He looked away and said gruffly, "I guess it can. It changed them."

Amy let go a small sigh and pushed back her chair. "I've got to go now," she said. "Sam needs more care than the doctor can give him. And by the way—he wants you to come and see him."

Embree wished that Amy would go and quit talking about Sam Arnim and Brad and Lily; he had a lot of thinking to do; let her go over and nurse Sam, so he, Embree, could rest.

He said shortly, "Tell him I'll be over tomorrow."

She was at the door when he remembered something. "What about Taos?" he asked.

Amy turned and looked at him gravely, and then she said, "I'm afraid I killed him, Embree." And she went out.

Not even his surprise could long endure at this moment, and he wondered only briefly that it had been Amy who had fired the shot he heard just before he lost consciousness; then he closed his eyes and slept.

Amy came in again in the evening, made some broth, and sat watching Embree gravely while he drank it. He felt better with it inside him, and he told her, "I'm feeling fit again—ready to travel. Might as well stir up and around a little."

Amy got up and picked up the bowl. "And fall right on your face? You stay right where you are, mister!"

He was easily convinced and slept like a log until the doctor came to change the bandage in the morning. The smell of coffee and bacon frying was through the house, setting the juices flowing in his jaws, and by the time the doctor closed his bag and left, Embree was famished. "You can get up," the doctor had said.

Amy appeared in the doorway, wearing an apron and holding a flapjack turner. She smiled at him and asked, "Hungry?"

"As a wolf."

"Then come on—I've got breakfast ready."

Still feeling a little woozy, still with a headache, he went to the kitchen, and after a breakfast of bacon and eggs and flapjacks, he began to feel better. While Amy cleared away the dishes he filled his pipe and lit it, the smoke tasting doubly good after this long time without it.

Amy watched him covertly while she worked at the sink. "Tom Houghton was in town, and he'll be back to see you." She laughed a small laugh. "Those farmers are going to make you mayor or governor or something, if you aren't careful. They're grateful—like all of us." And she squared around and looked directly at him, her blue eyes very still and grave.

After a moment he looked away. He didn't want any more of that. He said dryly, "Sorry I'll have to decline the nomination. Let's go see Sam."

He was thinking, as they walked along the boardwalk side by side in the warm sunshine, that the sooner he got out, the better. He had learned his lesson, but it was hard to steel himself against her; he had failed to do that once before and had almost been trapped by his own fantasies as a result.

They were on the doctor's porch, but Amy suddenly stopped near the door. She moved very close to him, her blue eyes widening and darkening as they searched his face.

She said, with soft firm resignation, "Jim Embree, I've given you every chance to change your mind about going away, but it looks like I'll have to take a hand." He felt her small soft hand reach out and grip his own, hard, as she moved even closer. "Why didn't you ever tell me—let me know?" she whispered. "I don't love Sam."

He couldn't find words at once. At last he said in a low unbelieving voice, "Are you sure, Amy? Sam said you'd promised to marry him."

She nodded. "He told me he said that, and told me why he had lied—to hurt you. And he told me something else——"

"Then I can speak, Amy?"

Slowly, her eyes crinkled up almost in laughter. "You don't have to," she said happily, surely. "Let's go inside."

Sam seemed thinner, and he was very pale, but as they came in he turned his face still unrelenting to Embree, his gray eyes watchful.

"How're you doing?" Embree asked.

Sam turned to Amy. "You tell him?" And at her nod, Sam said gruffly, "Embree, I don't like crow no matter how it's cooked, but I'll eat a little now. I was wrong about a couple of things, you included, and I was jealous." He hesitated, his eyes sharpening. "But some of the boys have been in, and they told me you could have left me there and everybody would have believed I was dead. I won't forget that."

"I almost did," said Embree softly.

"But you didn't." Sam looked at Amy. "You brought me back because you thought I meant the world and all to Amy." He paused once more. "Another one of my mistakes, too. But now, believe me or not, I'd like to be your friend. Think we could make it, Embree?"

They looked at one another, and then slowly Embree grinned, and Sam's face broke up and he smiled sheepishly.

"I'd sure like to try," Embree said honestly. "For myself, I think it'd be one of the easiest things I've ever done."

Sam stuck out his hand and Embree took it.

They went out then, and on the steps Embree stopped and looked at Amy, all at once thinking of the good future stretching ahead of them, his heart filling in a way that robbed him of all the things he wanted to say.

And then, being a neat man, who finished things when once he had started them, he said, "I've got to go send a wire to Joe Morrissey and tell him I won't be there. Want to come along?"

Amy beamed, and suddenly she leaned over and kissed him quickly and warmly on the lips, not caring in the least that they stood in broad daylight before the town of Wells.

"I do," she said, her eyes twinkling. "And I'll be that way from now on—I'll always want to come along, always want to be where you are, Jim. Like to change your mind before it's too late?"

He just looked at her, trying to say it, and then he put it all into one short phrase. "It was too late a long time ago." He reached out his hands and drew her, laughing, down the steps.

www.ingramcontent.com/pod-product-compliance
Lightning Source LLC
Chambersburg PA
CBHW030255270626
47156CB00022B/2774